seXdified

A Real Life Sex-Capade

mzScorpion & Lynx

authorHOUSE®

AuthorHouse™
1663 Liberty Drive
Bloomington, IN 47403
www.authorhouse.com
Phone: 1-800-839-8640

First published by AuthorHouse   06/06/2011

ISBN: 978-1-4567-6825-6 (e)
ISBN: 978-1-4567-6826-3 (dj)
ISBN: 978-1-4567-6827-0 (sc)

Library of Congress Control Number: 2011906960

Printed in the United States of America

ACKNOWLEDGEMENTS FROM MZSCORPION

I would like to thank God for placing this talent in my heart, because without him none of this would be possible. I want to thank all of the people who had faith in me and gave me a lot of support: Vickie Anderson, Katrice Johnson, Naiesha McNeill, Kevin Willis, Sukari, Miranda Sterling and Loticia Yates just to name a few and there are many more…

To my Grandmother Pearl, I know you will not read this book but I want you to know that I really appreciate all the talks and support you have given me with every phone call. No matter what I told I was doing you would tell me to follow my heart and dreams. Most people go to school for the talent I have within me. I thank you for the push and allowing my smile to be my umbrella.

To my niece Ti'aja Brennan you are my heart and I adore you. I love that I can be the role model you need in your life to keep you on your toes. You turned out to be such a wonderful young lady and I promise as long as I walk this earth you will be a very eminent and well-respected women. I love you. To my best friend (and chosen sister) Dee, I know these types of books make you blush and uncomfortable so I won't put you on blast. I also know you will always have my back for life and support me in all my crazy journeys. From day one God placed you in my life making us matching bookends and I could never express my gratitude enough. You helped me overcome some of the hardest tasks in my life and no matter how far away you may be, you will always be right in my heart. Love you forever.

To my Aunt/Mother Debbie Brennan, there are never enough words in this world to express my thanks for all your love and support. Your challenges with tough love helped to mold me into the women I am today.

I will be forever grateful. You are my aunt by relation but my mother by God and I know I only learned from the best. Thank you and I love you.

To my Lisa, Lisa Davis aka DJ China on the ones and twos…LOL. Taking on new challenges and facing them head on without fear is something I learned from you which gave me the strength to do this book. You have always been my guiding light, a leader, and role model but most importantly a wonderful Aunt. I could never thank you enough for all the support you give me each day. I love you more then you could ever know.

To my Business Consultant and Friend for life Shimi Stallings aka "The Shim." I want to thank you for all your help and support with teaching me how this game works. When you said you are "only a phone call away" you stuck by those words and made yourself available whenever I had a question. You are a good friend and my row dog for life. Thank you for being you.

To my editor Curtis Davis, even though it's been a while since we had our boxing match, I just want you to know I appreciate your help at such a short notice you are the freak'N best. P.S. be ready for a beat down… LOL…Hugs and Kisses.

To the best Author and partner in crime Lynx, I thank you for convincing me to write my stories. I was scared, feeling the pressure of not being good enough but you had faith that we could rock this out. I'm very happy I said "yes." You are a good friend and an amazing Author. I am so glad to have you in my life. I will be looking for your next novel "M.O.E."

Finally and most importantly; to my friend, counselor, coach, psychologist, teacher, and sex slave, my husband, Ty Bullock you are my muse. You always told me to publish my stories giving me a push every day. You had faith in me even when I told you that you were crazy. "I'm not a writer, plus I don't want people to know my thoughts." I said.

But, you inspired me with your wild and crazy imagination telling me to "let that inner freak out." I want you to know I appreciate you every day I breathe. I love you with all my heart. You are my rock!

Love Forever
mzScorpion

ACKNOWLEDGEMENTS FROM LYNX

For some reason I had a hard time writing my acknowledgements. There were a lot of people I wanted to thank but didn't want to offend anyone because of the contents of this book. It was fun writing this book with my co-author MzScorpion. I have no doubt in my mind you will enjoy all of the stories in SeXdified.

Now back to my acknowledgements. I first want to give honor to my Lord and Savior because without him I am nothing. He has given me the power of the pen as a talent to share with others. To my diva Alexus and handsome son CJ for making sure mommy had her time to write. Devine my little niece...love you! My nephew Deshawn for taking time out of his busy schedule to pose for the book cover and spreading the word about the book. To my other adopted nephews Marvel and Tareek, thanks for posing on the cover. The beautiful Elita (the chosen model for the book cover) you are a very talented young lady...keep doing your thing. The very talented photographer Virgil Brown, thanks for working with us and understanding our vision. I know we drove you crazy but thank you for your patience.

To my parents Bobby and Carolyn thanks for not judging me. I told you I wanted to write something for everyone to enjoy. My sister Del and brother Tony. My uncle J for trying to read AD-Dick... I still laugh about what you said. My friends for life Germaine Evans, Glenda Manuel, Crystal Talley, Latronia Maroney, Erika Gumbs, Danyell Hamilton. You ladies have seen the good and the bad but now prepare yourselves for the spectacular experience life is about to bring. I Love you ladies. Latronia Maroney we have work to do ...let's get it! To my hairstylists Myah and TayTay, two very talented women, thanks for keeping me looking fabulous! Miss Stir It Up LaTonya Taylor, thanks for having me on your show even when I didn't have a book out. To C-Stylz thanks for having my back! To my cousin Yar "Bloodline" Digg (Kenya.) Boy I crack up laughing when you asked "me where is Yasmine." Love you cuz for giving me your review.

To those who purchased my first book "Learning to Dance in the Storm", thank you so much for your support and the reviews. There is soooo much more to come!

To my family Hattie, Stanola, Jerome Williams, Leroy, Jerome Holmes, Sophia, Evelyn, Marvin, Shawnetta, Emonie, Camille, Tiffany, Shawn, Dennis, Jermaine, Ashley, Brenda, Charity, Jessica, Junie, Keisha, Gail, Lamont, Macio, Pat, Walter, Eric, ManMan, Dude, Luther, BJ, Tony, Pauline, Sheila, Bug, Chris, Janet, Shaquarna, and Charlene… Family means the world to me and I love you all so much. I dream big and next year we will be in Hollywood for our movie. Yeah, don't be shocked about anything that happens! And I can't forget my cousin on lock down Kee-Wee. Keep your head up and know your family will always be there for you. I can't wait to start on your story… Love you to life!

Last but not least, my girl MzScorpion none of this would be possible if I wasn't being so curious trying to find out what you were writing in the break room at HCA!… I went back to my desk and my brain started going a million miles over. I got the amazing, extraordinary idea and came over to your desk "hey let's write an erotica book together." The look on your face was priceless. God knew what he was doing when he put the two of us together. So watch out world MzScorpion and LYNX are on the move to devour and conquer!

All the SeXdified people in the world stand up!!!

Love and Peace!!!

Lynx

DELUSIONS OF A SEX FIEND

mzScorpion

It's a new day and I don't want to get out of bed. Here I lay thinking about how lonely I am. No friends to talk to; no man to lie next to at night or even argue with. It's not that I like to argue, but you know what I'm saying - can this be it for me? A single mom forever? Oh boy, life… is all I could think about as the alarm clock bellowed through the air at five o'clock in the morning. Urgggh! I reached over and hit the button to turn it off.

My name is Jordan Laker. I have a good job as a medical collections representative at one of the largest insurance companies in Virginia. I have three beautiful children, two boys and a girl. Sad to say I've never been married, or even close to it. Now, my kids all have the same father, which I am happy about. But, I regret it every day. Just the thought of him makes me sick. Sean and I met while on my way to school one morning. I was waiting on the #2 train at Nevins Street in Brooklyn, New York where I grew up. I remember him sitting on the bench looking so good with his wannabe-gangster, fly homeboys. How you trying to be cute and a gangster at the same time? Pick one dummies. Ok, so I was standing with my friend Sam talking about cheer practice when I saw him coming our way.

"He's coming… He's coming." I said interrupting her conversation.

"Who is coming?" Sam said.

"Dude with the big dark brown eyes, you know the cute one." I replied.

"So," Sam says in her arrogant voice. "Ok, just be cool, cause you know

1

he's coming over to ask me out, I knew he couldn't resist this right here," she bragged.

She was not pretty or shall I say the conventional TV, magazine pretty. But for some reason or another, guys were always asking her out. When he approached us I just moved to the side so they could talk but he moved in front of me and asked my name. I know I had a dumb look on my face when the words "huh you talk'N to me?" came out my mouth.

"Yes you the only one in front of me right now" he said.

"Hellooo you don't see me standing here you are rude," Sam said with her hand on her hips.

"Oh my bad, I didn't mean it that way, but I am standing right in front of your friend who has not given me her name yet. I'm Sean and you are?" he asked me again.

"I'm Jordan," I answered, with a big smile, and after that we were inseparable.

As the years went on I learned Niggas are always gonna be Niggas. Lying, cheating, abusive and everything in between. But my dumb ass kept messing with him anyway. I had my first son at age fifteen, My second son at nineteen and my baby girl at twenty-three years old. Now, I'm not saying I regret having my babies, I just wish I was married to the same man that fathered my children. And I wish he wasn't a fucking asshole! I used to dream of having a romantic wedding at night with candles that made the moon light shine so bright it look like you were standing right next to it. But that will never happen with him, I wouldn't do it even if you paid me. I left his ass after he brought me here to Virginia three years ago. He moved us here talking about "I want a better life for you, me and the kids." I found out a month after being here he had another child with some chick he cheated on me with. The little girl is the same age as our middle son… What a fucking beast. He moved us here so he could be closer to his daughter. Needless to say I have been celibate since. *I am so horny…Urggh*!

I got out of bed and began my daily routine by jumping in the shower then rubbing myself down with my favorite lotion, which is Banana Melon from Bath & Body Works. I put on my well-pressed clothes because that is how I do. Today's attire is a tan colored pencil skirt, royal blue lace bra and a white short sleeve blazer. My shoes of course are off the chain. I have a shoe fetish so I always have the hottest shit. I gave myself a glance over in the mirror that sits on my dresser… *got damn I am fine*! I walked down the hall to the boy's room "good morning boys, time to get up," I said as I flicked the light switch on.

"Time to get up for school. Lets go babies."

I crossed the hall to the "Lil Mama's" room, she is always the hardest to wake up.

"Ok mama, time to get up for school," I whispered, as I turned her light on and kissed her until she sat up. While they were getting ready I went into the kitchen to make breakfast so they can eat something before leaving the house. Doctors say "it is very important to have breakfast every morning." And breakfast is a good way to start a productive day.

While the children were eating, I gathered all our things and set them at the door. I went back to check the bedrooms and make sure all the lights were off when my phone rang. I already knew who it was before I answered

"Hello."

The voice on the other line replies "Hey there sexy lady what are you doing?"

"Sean it is seven in the morning what the HELL you think I'm doing?" I said with attitude. "Playing with yourself, thinking about daddy's thick dick" he said. I could hear the smirk in his voice.

"Never that!" I shouted in the receiver. "I have to go what the fuck you want?" He paused then said

"you know what I want so stop fronting DAMN."

I hung the phone up and walked back in the kitchen to make sure the little people were done and ready to go.

I piled everyone into the truck. Made sure they all had on their seat belts and we were off. The morning sun was parting through the clouds making the morning drive scenery look amazing. I pulled into the parking lot of the school to let the kids out. They jumped out, backpacks in hand, yelling "love you mommy have a good day." Kisses blowing in the wind. I yelled back "I love you, see you later and be good." I watched them run into the building along with other kids that were being dropped off by their parents. I pulled off taking the road with the hills to work.

The traffic seemed to be moving smoothly, so I should be on time. I decided to stop at 7-11 to get something to snack on while I'm at my desk. As I approached the light it turned red. I reached over to the radio to turn it up. You know the best time to hear your favorite jam's is when you are alone in the car. "Invented Sex" by Trey Songs was playing. This is my joint, I mumbled to myself. For some reason that song made me wet every time. I could see it now, Trey pulling back the sheets so I can climb on top of him. Umm…Umm…Umm. I closed my eyes, biting my bottom lip while singing the song as if I was being blessed, knowing I looked crazy. I turned my head and noticed a black Toyota Camry next to my truck at the light. The driver was a chocolate, bald headed brother wearing a light grey dress shirt with a navy blue and white tie. Good God he is fine, I remember thinking. He turned his head in my direction and smiled then waved hi. I just smiled back and turned my head noticing the light was now green. I drove off still headed to the 7-11, which was just ahead on my right. I turned into the parking lot and pulled up to a spot right at the front door. I threw the truck in park, jumped out and went inside.

Of course, I wanted some candy, so that's what I went to find. I was in the hard candy aisle when I heard.

"I see you like to sing Mrs…"

I turned and there he was the sexy dude from the red light.

"Excuse me?" I said, stunned he was standing there.

"I said, I see you like to sing Mrs…" he repeated.

"It's Jordan but without the Mrs." I replied.

"Cute Jordan, I'm Eric. So what song were you jamming to so hard, like you were getting it in?" he asked with a smirk.

I just laughed with the look of embarrassment on my face. I put my Twizzlers on the counter and passed the cashier five bucks. Once she handed me my change I turned to the guy and told dude to have a good day. I walked out of the 7-11 and got back into my truck. What in the world was I doing? I need to be nice, he might give me some dick. Just as I put the car in reverse, he came right out and walked over to my truck. He must have been 6 foot 2 with a medium build, but fine as hell.

"So, cute Jordan, do you have a number?" he asked.

"Why should I give you my number?" I said, putting the gear back in park. *Don't judge me, I said I'm having withdraws right now.*

"I see you every morning at the same light, singing," He said, "so when I saw you come in here, I figured this would be the perfect time to talk to you. So… what do you say? Can we get to know each other?"

Is he for real! Should I do it? I guess it couldn't hurt.

"I'll give you my number and we can see what happens from there is that cool?" I asked.

He just smiled.

I reached over to my bogo bag on the passenger seat to get a pen and something to write on. I found a business card from the cleaners. I wrote my cell number and name on it.

"Here you go, you can call me any time after six" As I turned back around to hand him the card, but he was walking away. "Chaaa." I sucked my teeth. I knew this was a fucking joke. I rolled my eyes and tossed the card on the passenger seat when he yelled

"hay let me give you my number as well."

"Oh ok," I said with excitement reaching, back over to pick up the card I just tossed on the seat.

Yeah I know I got upset, but got damnit I'm human, and a female… Shit, that's what we do!

I got out of the truck, walked over to his car and handed him the card. He was writing his number on a napkin, so I leaned on the hood of his Camry waiting for him to finish.

"Here you go cute Jordan" he said as he smiled then came close to me. "I like what you are wearing" He whispered as he gently pushed his pelvis into mine… "and you smell real nice. What is that?"

"I'm sure you would like to know but in due time my friend, in due time" I mumbled.

"Oh, really you want to play hard to get? Well let me show you something" as he slid his hand up my thigh until it was completely covered by my skirt.

"Oooh… you one of those females" he said, noticing I was panty-less.

Taking his thumb and index finger to spread my lips apart and using his middle finger to find my woman-hood, he began fingering me.

"Oooh so wet, I like that" he whispered in my ear.

He began to unzip his pants. I raised my eyebrows like did he just? He released the beast that was fighting to get out. Wow he's not working with a lot but let's see. He spun me around, pushed my back down causing me to bend over. I began to shake. This was electrifying. Fucking in a parking lot in broad daylight. He entered me ever so gently. With each stroke I could feel my eyes rolling in the back of my head. I began to tremble from the sensation. Ok, so he knows how to use it.

He started barking "sweet!…sweet!…sweet!"

Then it dawned on me, it was the sound of horns beeping for me to move, the light had turned green and I was just sitting there. OMG! Here we go… Delusions.

CHAPTER 2

I arrived at work ten minutes early as usual. I walked into my office, turned on the computer and began checking my emails. "Morning, Morning" I could hear the girls greeting each other as they came in. I looked up and noticed Tiffany, one of the collection Reps on my team, standing at my office door.

"Good morning Jordan. How are you?" She said, smiling.

"Morning Tiffany, I'm fine and yourself?" I responded, not really wanting to know the answer.

"I'm good. Wonderful day today, 'its hump-day'" she said in a seductive voice as she chuckled. "Just can't wait, two more days till Friday, then you know I'm gowina hit the club! Gurl you should come wit me it'z gowina be off da chain" Tiffany said, getting totally excited.

"Thanks for the invite, but I will have the kids this weekend…*sorry*" I replied with a fake sad face.

"Aight well, if you change your mind, you know my numba. Let me get to my desk; see you later gurl." She walked off and I just shook my head thinking she is so country.

This was not going to be a good day. Here I am so horny because I haven't had sex in three years and she talk'N bout "hump day." Who the hell does that? Anyway, I began working on reviewing accounts and making phone calls. To help me get started I turned on my I-pod and worked until lunchtime. Staying focused is the key. It was time to eat and my stomach was screaming for food. I made it a point to bring lunch with me every day so I can save some cash and not be distracted by any sexiness that may be lurking in McDonalds, Wendy's or wherever. I went to the restroom. I hate this damn bathroom, these females are so fucking nasty. How is it that I can smell your *cunt* when I enter the bathroom but you can't smell it (or so they pretend not to smell that shit) and it's right under your nose? I used the toilet, washed my hands and went back to my office.

It was a PB&J day. This is the best time to relax… lunchtime. I took my PB&J out and reached down to turn on the chair massager. Ahhh! I leaned back and closed my eyes. As the chair vibrated up and down my spine, it was causing some tingling in my you know where. Ummm… the feeling was so good. My mind drifted to the guy from the red light and I imagined him licking me real slow causing my grape to swell with pleasure. The moans got louder as I drifted into a zone. I started grinding my pussy real slow to catch the rhythm of the massager. I grab the handles as if it was his head, making sure to keep him in the right place because it was coming. I was Cuming and Cuming. I took deep breaths trying to gain restraint. It was so good that the muscles in my stomach tightened up causing my body to jerk. I needed to relax before someone came in. I was breathing like I just did the 10K. I reached over the side of the chair and turned that bad boy off. I laid my head on my desk feeling like I needed to take a nap. Now you know when you get sleepy, that nut was good. I rested for a minute just to make sure my legs were not shaking, then I stood up. Whew!

Feeling so relieved, I took my bathroom bag out of the bottom draw and went to the bathroom to clean myself off. That should get me through the rest of my day. As the day came to a close I was rushing out of the office like a bat out of hell so I can pick up the kids at the YMCA. It seems like everybody leaves the office at the same time. This parking lot is always congested. Finally I reached the YMCA. I ran inside hoping I was not too late.

"Good evening Mrs. Laker" the after-school teacher said. "We are having our parents date night this Friday, in two more days." She said smiling. Why she say "in two more days" like I don't know what today is. "The kids will be able to stay until nine o'clock PM while you and the hubby enjoy the evening together" the teacher continued.

"Okay, thank you" I told her and walked down the steps to get the kids. I tapped on the glass and waved toward them. All three of them jumped up running to the door and wrapped their hands around my waist.

"Hey babies how was ya'll day?" Sean Jr., my oldest, just smiled while the other two asked what was for dinner. I was too busy thinking about what that teacher said. How could she think I was married? Has she ever seen me with a man? Or, ever seen any men come here to pick up my kids? Oh well, maybe she think I'm married to the kid's father. I laughed to myself. Slow ass.

"What's so funny mama?" Sean Jr. asked.

"Oh nothing baby, just thinking about something that's all. Ok, let's go, I have to cook dinner."

My mind drifted back to their dick-head father. He was the fucking worst. Married to him? Not even if I was in a mental asylum. That teacher was mad. I got the kids in the truck and headed home. It was late and I was done for the day. When we got home I told the kids to make sure they get their homework out so I can check it while I prepared dinner. Tonight's menu: pineapple glazed chicken breast with yellow rice and baby carrots. With the kids all bathed and homework checked it was time to eat.

"Mommy this smells wonderful" Jr. said. He was always saying things to make me smile. At dinner, they all got a chance to tell one thing about their day whether it was good or bad. It is something I like to do for family time. More parents should do this because you would be surprised at what transpired during your child's day.

Once diner was all done I sent the kids to bed. I cleaned the kitchen, took my shower and climbed into bed myself. I turned on the TV, but as always, nothing was on but the news. My mind began to wonder again, causing my body temperature to rise, so I did what I do best and let my hands do their dance around the curves of my breasts. They were plump like cantaloupes with hard nuts in the center. My nipples were so erect you, could snap them right off. The left hand found its way to my pool of sweet sauce. I began to make small circles around my clit allowing my middle finger to guide itself in and out the tunnel, while the other hand pinched and mauled my breast. I began to shiver like a wet mouse. I adjusted both my legs up and spread them open to get into the motion. My hands were so wet from the sugary sweetness I had to taste it. Wow I really am sweet. Ummm… moaning was like a second language for me. More… more… I sang to myself and I really needed more. I wanted to be overwhelmed with pleasure, so I stopped what I was doing and leaned over the side of my bed. I shoved my hand between the mattress and box spring until I located "Scott" my boy toy. I leaned back on my pillows then turned *him* on. Scott started rumbling slow then faster, just like I like it. I helped him locate my center world and he wiggled and swayed against my walls making me yearn for more. So I switched the bird to hum and glided Scott in and out. Each time it went in, the bird kissed my clit. I must have been hyperventilating because the room started spinning and I was so hot, steam was coming out my ass. I started thrusting my body as I rocked my hips causing major friction. I threw my head back and bit my bottom lip as I jerked uncontrollably from the eruption. Heavy breathing escaped my lungs from such a pleasurable moment. I was so ready to fall asleep. I relaxed my body to savor the moment.

CHAPTER 3

"Another day another damn dollar" is how they say it right? I reached over, turned off the alarm clock and repeated the same routine. Shower, get dressed, get the kids ready, off to school, then work. Today had to be a better day. Shit, it's just one more day til Friday. I sat at my desk, turned on the desktop and picked up the phone to check for any stupid ass voice messages. Thank God no complaints. Whew! So I started my workload. Determined to enjoy my work for the first time, I turned on the massager and sat back in my chair. Ok I know that is not work, but like I keep telling you, I need some dick. A knock on the door broke my concentration... "Yes? Come in," I said. And the bullshit begins…. "Excuse me Mrs. Laker, I have an Insurance Rep on the line who wants to make a complaint," the reception said. Why do they keep calling me Mrs? They know I don't have a husband. "Sure, give me a second. Which line is it?" I asked. "Line two," she said, closing the door. "Ok thanks." When the door was closed I turned off the massager, stood up, adjusted my skirt, then sat back down.

"Ahhumm" clearing my throat as I picked up the line and began speaking. "Good afternoon, this is Ms. Laker, how can I help you?"

Immediately the Rep started yelling. "Your staff is very rude, always getting smart when they call, then talking to my department like we dumb. I am very sick of it and want you to handle it right now!"

"I sure will, can you please tell me what happened?" I asked, rolling my eyes because of her attitude.

"Your collection Rep Erica, said 'listen I need you to tell me why this claim is not paid and I don't wanna be on hold for a long time got it?'"

"I am so sorry that she treated your Rep that way. I will have a talk with her right now. I assure you it will not happen again, I said. But if there is ever another problem, please let me know."

"Thank you for your understanding. I sure will and you have a good day" and hung up.

I hung up the phone then called Erica's extension. She answers "Yes?"

"Please come see me in my office. NOW!"

Seconds later Erica knocked on the door.

"Come in and have a seat. Can you please tell me what happened on that last call before I pulled it?" I asked Erica. "Well first off, that Rep took a long time to pick up the line and I needed to go to the bathroom. They always have you on hold for a long time and I just didn't want to wait… like I said I had to go to the bathroom." Erica replied with attitude. I didn't let her finish because clearly she is out her damn mind.

"Umm, well let me tell you how this works. That type of behavior is not tolerated," I said. "Consider this as your verbal warning. Got it?" I just wanted to get to the point.

"Yeah, sure" with her lips curled like a rebellious child.

Erica left the office and I was pissed the hell off. That damn girl ruined my nut. As the day continued I received several calls from other insurance companies about claims. It became a busy day and before I knew it, it was five o'clock, time to leave the office. I rushed out of there to get the kids from the Y and headed home… I needed a drink. On the way home my cell phone started going off. I answered "hello."

"Where the HELL are my kids?" the voice on the other end barked.

"OMG! Well, hello to you too" I said, "they are right here and we are on the way home. If you can give me a half hour I will have them call you back." I replied, then I hung up. I hate my kid's father he makes my skin crawl. As I pulled into the drive way my cell was ringing again. Of course it was Sean. This dumb fuck doesn't understand time… I said half hour, it was only twelve damn minutes. I didn't even pick up I just went in the house and had the kids do their usual. They can call him tomorrow. This has been a long day. Lights out!

Morning again, and time for work. Same routine every day but the best thing about today is it's Friday and I get to leave work early. I arrived at work ready to leave. I know I just walked in but I didn't want to be there. I checked my email. URGENT meeting, attendance from the big boss. *Please attended Change Meeting at 10:00AM all employees must be present.* Blah, I so don't feel like sitting in a meeting on Friday. Boring! Well, at least my day will go by real quick. I began calling on unpaid claims, fussing with the insurance companies and checking payments that have posted to make sure they zeroed out when Tiffany tapped on the door and asked. "It's time for the meeting, I'm going over now, do you want me to save you a seat?" "Yeah sure I'll be right there, I have to get my things" I grunted. Tiffany didn't move. Instead, she just stood there watching me get ready. I grabbed a note pad and a retractable pencil, closed my office door and we headed down the hall to the large conference room on site B. Tiffany came out of nowhere with "that dress looks real good on you, I like that material, it's jersey right?" "Yes it is" I replied. Tiffany always admired what I wore. She was a real nice looking girl but could not dress for shit. I felt sorry for her. I should take her shopping with me to buy the right kinda clothes that would make her look sexy.

We entered the large conference room and sat down in the last row in the back, closest to the door. The meeting was just starting. Edwin Murry is one of the "Top Dogs" in the company and he was conducting the meeting. He's about five foot nine, low hair cut, chestnut brown skin tone with full plump lips that revealed the most beautiful straight white teeth. Well, almost straight. His right front tooth was slightly chipped which made him look even more seductive. I would like to suck his dick! Ok...ok I know I'm tripping.

Anyway, he is so sexy. The yummiest piece of eye candy that anyone could have telling them what to do. I'd do whatever you want daddy, just say it, I thought as he walked back and forth in front of the room talking about what? I have no clue. I was not paying attention. Every chick in the office knew they would never have a chance with him. He never gave me or any other female the time of day. He let us all know he was happily gay and proud of it. What a lucky man he has at home. I bet his ass is fine too.

After about an hour, the meeting was over and Tiffany said to me, "I know you are leaving for the day, so I was wondering if you could give me a ride since my car is in the shop. I was gonna call my momma and have her come get me but I would have to wait like an hour before she would get here. She is so damn slow." Now listen, I have taken this girl home so many times on Friday, it's not even funny. But I will say that every time I took her home, she gave me ten dollars for gas. I said "sure, you can meet me out front." I didn't need the money, but took it anyway. Don't turn up your face to me, you know damn well you would take the fucking money too. We met in front of the building and headed to my truck. Tiffany is a talker, so I never say a word, I just listen or pretend I'm listening. As I opened the door I shrieked "what the hell was that?" I felt something hit my arm. Tiffany jumped and frowned her face. "Ewww bird shit is all down the side of your arm, in your hair and down your back." This is some B.S. I told Tiffany I would have to go home first and take a quick shower to wash this shit out of my hair before I dropped her off at her boyfriends. She said "sure, whatever, beggars can't be choosey." We got in the truck and started driving. I was having a hard time trying to drive because I didn't want to smear the bird crap all over me or in my truck.

When we pulled in the driveway I parked the truck, jumped out real fast and ran to unlock the door. I ran in the house and yelled to Tiffany "make yourself at home while I take my shower." I turned on the shower then slowly took of my clothes trying not to touch the poop. I stepped in the water and started washing my body. Yuck, this was so nasty and embarrassing. I picked up the shampoo squeezed some in my hand, wet my hair and rubbed it in. As it lathered up, I was enjoying the scent. I always used Pantene, the one in the brown bottle. I rinsed my hair and turned off the shower. I reached out to grab my towel when I heard Tiffany say "may I have one of these waters?" She went in my fridge WHAT THE FUCK? "sure." I walked out of the bathroom into my bedroom where Tiffany was looking at the lotions on my dresser. "Now I know why you always smell so good," she said. Hmmm ok. I sat on the edge of my bed with the towel wrapped around me. I reached over to pick up my banana melon body lotion, but it fell out my hand and rolled under my bed. Damn. Tiffany said "oh I can get it for you." She bent down in front of me and looked under the bed. "Ok, ok I got it" As she got up she stopped and traced her index finger up my left leg to my inner thigh. I looked at her and she gave me a gaze. "Your skin is so soft" she said. "Uhhh what are you doing" I asked but never moved her hand. Then it felt like a hot breeze rushed into my bedroom. Tiffany licked my inner thigh. She touched my cream and asked if she could have a taste of my center world. She pulled my towel gently to reveal my fruits from the forbidden tree. I gasped not knowing what to do next. She pushed me back slowly and opened my legs so softly I felt weak. She placed her head between my thighs. She said "ummm you have a very enticing aroma" then slid her tongue in my soft spot. I inhaled and closed my eyes. Is this really happening?

This girl must be a pro because I was feeling like jelly. She must always go down south. She knew every road like it was her own. When she reached my house, I just swung the door right open. I was running like a raging river. It was out of control. There was no beaver dam to block the flow. I started flopping like a fish gasping for air. She got up and wiped her mouth then pulled her pants down Wow, no panties, just like me, "commando." Anyway she climbed on top of me, raised my right leg and placed her pussy on mine. We made slow rocking motions rubbing our twats together. I reached up allowing my hands to guide their way up her shirt to her breast, they felt like "Cottonall" tissue. We moved our hips in a rhythm, as if we were singing a song in harmony. Then she said "Jordan is it ok?"

"Yes…Yes…Yes…it is" I groaned.

"Sorry?" I said can I have a water? Tiffany replied.

"Oh… yes, you can have the water it is fine, I will be ready in a minute."

Shit… I can't believe I was day dreaming again what the hell is wrong with me?

Tiffany walked back in the living room. I closed my door and sat on my bed. As I rubbed my lotion on, all I could think about was how I really need to get a man, I am so backed up it's not even funny. I threw on some skinny leg jeans, a Mickey tee and some black baby doll flats. Brushed my hair back in a ponytail and went in the living room.

"You ready" I said as she got up from the small arm chair.

"You look like a little girl" she said with a smile.

"I guess that is a compliment" I said smiling back at her.

"Of course, not many women can look that good after having three kids I hope I look like you when I have kids," Tiffany said.

"Thank you."

We left the house and I drove her to her boyfriends. Tiffany asked me to wait while she went to get the money from him. I told her she could give it to me on Monday, but she insisted. so I waited. A few seconds later, a short stocky Italian dude came out and started walking toward my car. When he approached me he said "sup gurly," nodding his head in a hello fashion. He was wearing a tight white muscle shirt and blue jeans. He looked just like the dude Ronnie from that TV show "Jersey Shore."

"Hey how are you." I smiled and nodded.

"Yeah so ahhh, Tiff said you need ten dollars? Here you goes."

Yep, he's a Guido.

"Ok, thank you" I said. "Is she coming back out?"

"Naw she's in the batroom. You can go I'll tell her you will see her Monday" he said turning to walk away.

"Okay… Tell her I said thanks."

I drove off and headed towards Chesterfield Town Center Mall to look around for a little bit before picking up the kids. I love coming here during this time of day because no one is here except old people and the mommy & me groups. Those mothers have it made. Sometimes I wish I was a Stay At Home mom. Yeah right! I would lose my got damn mind. Look at them, just sitting around watching their kids play, pretending to like each other. I walked into Old Navy not looking for anything important, just killing time. They had the cutest skirts for my daughter so I had to get them. I was checking out some shirts when these two guys caught my attention. They had on the same outfit, which I thought was odd. What kind of adults wear the same outfits? That is so elementary school, I thought. They were looking at the men's swimwear, picking them up and sizing them too each other. I could not understand what they were saying. They were not speaking English. I'm thinking French. Yeah, I was being nosy, you do the same thing. I walked closer so I could see what they looked like. As I got closer they turned around. Oh snap they were twins. They both smiled and said hello to me. I forced a smile and wave hi back. The two of them could have been bookends. I wanted to melt. Big, bold eyes, olive skin and curly hair. They were sexy. I picked up two pair of swimming trunks and headed to the dressing room. I went in the second room and sat down. I was not buying the swimming trunks but I had to get away from the twins. Moments later I heard them come in, laughing. They went into the fitting room next to mine. I could hear his zipper pulled down and pants hit the floor. I wanted to see the goods so I stood on the little bench and looked over the divider. Only one of them was in there trying on a pair Speedos. The other one was outside waiting. Oh shit! He saw me. "Excuse me, what are you doing?" The one outside the fitting room asked me. I jumped down.

"I'm so sorry" I said as I opened the door to run out.

"It's ok he smiled, maybe you can help us pick the right swimming trunks." The one that was inside opened the fitting room door and stood there with his hands on his hips.

"So what you think?" he asked me. First, that accent made my pussy drop to my feet then the sight of his dick in those little ass shorts, whew!

"Ah… maybe you need a bigger size" I suggested.

"You think so?" he said, then removed them right in front of his brother and me. The one in the doorway said something in French *"Vous aimez ce que vous voyez?"*

"Sorry didn't get that?" I said, looking at him like he was crazy.

16

"I said, you like what you see?" he repeated in English. At that point it didn't matter because I was already turned the fuck on.

"Hell yeah" I said real loud, realizing I was acting hyped up.

"So then join us" he said.

The three of us stood so close in that little ass space. We stripped out of our clothes (well just two of us did) and I asked them if they liked what they saw. *"Oh, oui je vous remerice!" they replied in unison.* That was it, I was done … *Fuck me now.* I got down on my knees, taking both of their cocks in hand. I Licked on them like ice cream cones, from one to the other, then tried to shove them in my mouth at the same time. They played in my hair while holding my head in place, pumping their hips in and out like an acoustic sound wave. Sounds of pleasure escaped the dressing room. I allowed myself to enjoy one while stroking the other. I obeyed each throb from every vein as it massaged the moist flesh of my cheeks forcing it as far back in my throat until my uvla tickled his urethra. They groped my sweaty pillows. I stopped sucking long enough for one to get behind me while the other stood in front of me. The pumping motion was causing my head to bob and weave. I could not believe this shit was going down. I devoured his fuck stick like it was a beef jerky. Lips smacking, juice slurping, skin tapping, nuts busting.

"Hello, are you ok?" I heard a voice say in the distance.

Oh my God, was I really having an episode right here in the middle of the store?

They asked again "are you ok? Can we help you?"

I dropped the clothes I had in my hands and ran out of the store.

CHAPTER 4

It was just about time for me to pick up the little people. I took out my cell phone and called *dumb ass* to see if he would like the kids for the weekend so maybe I can have some me time. Why did he say "what do I get for babysitting for you?" What the hell you mean "baby sit?" These are your kids too stupid, you don't baby sit.

"Well you should give me some ass, plus you know you want too, he said with his little smirk. Then maybe I will watch them over night."

"First Sean, I would never let you touch this pussy, ever again or just to look at it. Even if you were the last Gynecologist on earth! Now, do you want to see your kids for the weekend? Yes or no?" I said in the driest tone I could muster.

He just said "come on Jordan, don't be like that. You know I can blow your back out just like you like. It's been a long time."

"Sean, get a fucking grip. Every time I laid down with you I had a child and an STD, so no fucking thanks. Now answer the question yes or no?" I said.

"Fine Jordan, have it your way. I can't take them tonight, I'm not going to be home."

Sean is so full of shit. I was mad as hell. But not because he wasn't going to take the kids, I was mad because he was right. I would have loved for him to fuck the shit out of me. Even though I hated him with every bone in my body, the dick was off the chain. First, the size of his dick looked like it belonged to a donkey. Second, it was smooth like caramel and when it was erect it was gorgeous, just so sexy. Now, I know you don't say a dick is pretty but Happy Jesus!

He would slide it in my pussy and I would shiver right away. You would have thought that dick had a mind of its own the way it moved all by itself. It was like my pussy was the remote control. At least that is how it felt to me. I was getting wet just thinking about it.

I hung up on Sean and went in the YMCA. When I walked in, the after school class was outside playing on the field. I looked around for my little people.

"Good afternoon Mrs. Laker" the teacher yelled from the swings.

I just waved as my kids came running toward me. Oh boy here she comes I thought to myself as she walked over to me. "Are the kids staying for parents night out?" she asked, smiling. Don't she see the look on my face? *Hellooo… I'm here picking them up… duh!*

"No, they are not staying. Thank you" I said and tried to walk away but she followed me.

"I thought you and your husband were going out?"

Nosey, annoying little bitch. "No I never said that, sorry" I said trying to force a smile through my gritting teeth. What the hell is she still following me for? It was none of her business.

"Well, you guys should. Every parent needs some time for themselves," she said. Ok now she is pissing me off. If I turn around and punch her in the fucking head I would be wrong, right? I put the kids in the truck and told her we will see her Monday and to have a good weekend, ignoring her comment. What has my life become? I have no man and my cunt is so tight I need a can opener to crack this bad boy open just to piss.

I took the kids to the movies so they wouldn't be bored and I could clear my head. Even though it was Friday, it was still early so the crowd had not come in yet. I got our tickets and went to the concession counter.

"May I get three kids packs?" I asked the chic behind the register. The kids were reading a poster for a movie about owls soon to be released when the girl behind the counter said

"So you want three kid packs?" I just figured she didn't hear me the first time and I repeated myself. But no, that was not the case.

"What size popcorn you want for the kids?" she asked.

"I thought they only came in one size, as a deal with a drink and candy" I said in a cynical voice.

"Well, the only thing that comes like that are the kids packs. Would you like that?" she asked me, for the second time. Rolling my eyes, "YES!"

"How many?"

Huhhh!, gritting my teeth I explained one more time, "listen, I want

THREE kids packs please." I made sure I didn't yell, but she was taking me there.

"Ok, no problem" she said.

What the hell is wrong with people? Am I the only one with common sense? I had the boys pick up their boxes as I took the one for my daughter and we walked into towards our theatre. The guy taking the tickets was cute but not all that. The one thing he did have going for him, and that I really liked, were his eyes, they were hazel.

"Hello, welcome to Common Wealth 20," he said as we approached.

His voice was so full of base a chill hit me in the back on my neck when he spoke.

"Are these your kids?" He asked.

"Yes these are my babies," I said, handing him the tickets.

"Well, you look like a baby yourself" he said, smiling at me.

Umm, ok, smooth, "thank you."

He asked the kids what their names were. I took it upon myself to answer with their names, plus I always tell my kids not to speak to strangers so they were just staring at him.

"You guys are so cute," he said smiling. "Oh, and I can't forget you little miss lady. So what is mommy's name?" "Jordan!" I said.

He immediately followed up with "and, does Jordan have a number?" Bold, I thought.

"We have to get in the movie" I said, as I smiled, flashing my half of dimple in my right cheek and walked away. I know… go ahead and say it, why didn't I give him my number if I keep complaining I need a man? I had my kids with me and that shit is not cool.

During the movie, I went out to the bathroom, not really needing to use it, but hoping to see the dude.

"Hi again" he said as I walked past him.

"Now that you are alone, how bout that number?" He asked.

I said "Ok here you go" and he took out his cell. I recited my number to him then he did the same. I walked away, but slow enough so he could get a good view of my ass. Yes, all women do it. Some more than others, but we love when a man looks as we walk away. I went to the bathroom and just stood in the mirror looking at my body. Checked my face to make sure no crust was in my eyes or little people in the window. I washed my hands and went back to the movie. That night was so boring, but the kids had plenty of fun. After putting them to bed, I went out into the backyard with a book and a glass of wine. I laid in my hammock and watched the stars.

This would be the life if I had a husband to lay here next to me, kissing my neck and saying how much he adores me. I was swaying in the wind, day dreaming, when my butt started humming. I jumped from the vibration. It was my cell. Who the hell is calling me at midnight? I thought.

"Hey lil mama what are you doing?" Why did I answer the phone?

"What Sean it is late?" I said, now agitated I picked up the call.

"I'm here at your door ready to pick up the kids" he said. Are you fucking kidding me?

"HELL TO THE NO. They are asleep and you don't just pop up at my damn door. I said. Plus, you said you were not going to be home. Call me tomorrow and I'll see if you can get them" I said.

"Oh well, since they sleep and I'm here how bout you let me hit dat?" he said

"Didn't we have this conversation earlier? Like what the fuck is wrong with you?" I asked him.

"Yo what is wrong with you…you be bugging?" He seemed pissed.

"Go the hell on, and don't ring my door bell or knock, bye." I hung up on him again.

Men be tripping.

CHAPTER 5

I could feel him breathing down the back of my neck. His breath smells like Bubblelicious gum. Tracing the curves in my spine with his index finger as the warm water cascaded down my breast. His pubic hair tickled my butt cheeks while he let me feel what he was working with. I wanted him inside me so bad but he continued to tease me with friction. I leaned close to the shower knobs as I arched my back to raise my ass letting him know I was inviting his pleaser piece to swirl around my joyful sin.

TLC's, "Red Light Special" played in the background, making the moment more enticing. He slid his middle finger in my pussy and my moans grew louder with each glide. His dick was saluting, as if my body was its drill sergeant. Then he removed his hands and slowly bent down taking my left leg and putting it up on his knee. He opened my apple bottom letting his tongue dance back and forth from my peach to my apple. He "Ummmed" and "Ahhhed" as he enjoyed the fruits I placed before him. "Turn around" he said in that deep voice. I spun around like I was a ballerina. I opened my legs and straddled him. As I lowered myself on top of him, his dick rose to meet me. I rode that man like he was a mechanical bull. I just knew I was a pro. His hands played in my hair as the water fell on the both of us. He licked each breast like lollypops. I began to cum so I went faster and faster. When I was done I got up but it was not over he turned me around and made me touch my toes. This was new for me. All of it. I bent over and wanted to yell. The feeling was so over whelming my legs became rubber. He started to pound me like some steak. My head hit the wall a few times when it dawned on me. It was the door. "Just a second" I yelled out. It was my middle son. He was letting me know that my cell phone was ringing. "Ok baby I will get it when I get out." I was taking a shower after we cleaned the house, it was the usual for a Saturday in my house. I finished cleaning myself and got out. These delusions are getting out of control. I wrapped a towel around myself and walked into my bedroom. I closed the door and picked up my phone off the bed to see who called. Oh my god. It was him, the guy from the movie theater. I pressed the green phone icon and listened as it ranged. The voice on the other end picked up.

"Hello, this Ryan." I closed my eyes and said

"Hi Ryan this…" is but he cut me off.

"I know, Jordan. I was wondering if you would call me back," he said, with his deep ass voice. "Sorry I didn't leave a message. Can you talk?"

I said "sure what's up?"

"How was your night?" He asked.

"It was cool and yours?"

"Well I couldn't sleep because you were on my mind" he said. He so full of shit.

"Oh really, you don't even know me like that" I said.

"I would like to get to know you. The only thing I know is that you have three gorgeous kids and you were not rocking a wedding ring. Am I right?" He asked. So he was paying attention, I like that he was observant like I am.

"Yes that is all true." I asked him if he had a girl or as men say "friend." When he said he was married, the air in my body felt as if it were being sucked right out of me, like when Freddy Kruger grabbed that girl and asked '*You wanna suck face?*' in 'Nightmare on Elm Street.'"

"We are separated. I haven't been with her for four months, so there is nothing to worry about" he said confidently. I was not comfortable with that because you all know how that works. I told him I had to get dressed and I will call him back. He knew I was lying but was like "ok."

I put lotion on my whole body. Then I went downstairs to make the kids lunch. I turned on the computer to check my email to see what was popping on Facebook. Of course you know people on Facebook just talk garbage, so I was catching up on the bullshit. Some of it was funny but others just get on my damn nerves. I had just told the kids to go in the back yard and play when the doorbell rang. No need for you to ask who was at the door because you already know. I opened the door and told him to come in. I called the kids from the backyard. "Daddy" they yelled while running to him. "Hey babies how ya'll doing? he said hugging them all simultaneously. Ya'll wanna go with me to a cookout at uncle Malakis'?"

"Yeah, can we mama?" They asked excitedly.

"I will go get their things. What time are you bringing them back?" I asked.

He said he was not sure, it was an engagement cookout because Malaki was getting married. I said tell him congratulations and went to get the kids stuff. I gave the kids five bucks each and a sweater. I kissed each of them as they walked out the door. The dumb fuck says "can I get a kiss too?" "Get out my face," I said, as I closed the door.

Since I had nothing to do, I called Ryan back to see what he was up to. *Don't judge me. So what, I said I wasn't gonna call but I was bored.* He picked up on the second ring.

"Hey boo."

"Hahaha, I'm not your boo," I laughed.

"My bad," he said. "So what's up?"

I laid across my sofa to get comfortable.

"So tell me about yourself."

We talked for two hours. It was so nice to have an adult conversation. He made me hot and wet. I loved his voice, it should be on the radio. His phone battery died which ended our call. I turned on the TV. The movie "Brothers" was on. I would fuck the shit out of Morris Chestnut, you have no idea. Those lips. Oooh! Just give me one night. I got up and went in the kitchen to get an ice cream snicker bar out the freezer. I need a life, I thought, when my cell went off. It was Ryan again.

"Hey again Miss Lady, what are you doing?"

"Nothing just watching TV" I replied.

"Would you like some company?" He asked.

I said "sure but not at my place, if you want I can come to your place."

I don't play people coming to my house like that. I have kids and that would be putting them in danger. What if dude was crazy? Naw I'm good. He said "yeah that would be cool, let me give you my address." I wrote it down and jumped in the shower again. I rubbed my banana melon lotion all over my body, even my cunt. *Hey, you never know.* I put on some black Dereon jeans, a black Dereon tee with hot pink graphics and my black and pink uptowns. I called Ryan to let him know I was on my way. It took me about ten minutes to get to his place. I was feeling unsure as to whether or not I should be here, but what the hell, I was there already.

He opened the door as I parked next to his car in the driveway. He was smiling like the Kool-Aid man. When I got out he was like "aww... you look like a little girl. I like that you are so versatile with your appearance. I bet if you wanted you could look like cat women and sneak up on me and take my virginity." I just smiled. His place was real nice. You could tell he lived alone but then again you never know right? It was a country style cottage. He had masculine furniture, you know the kind with dark cherry wood, a cocoa brown, leather living room set and a large flat screen TV. I would say about 50." We went into the living room and he sat on the sofa. I sat in the armchair.

"Would you like something to drink?" he asked looking at me crazy.

"Sure do you have bottle water?" I replied. When he got up he said

"you don't have to sit so far away I'm not gonna, bite unless you want me to." He had on a Tee shirt and some sweat pants. I could see his penis bulging through his sweats as if he stuffed a sock in there.

"Ummm" I said not realizing it was not in my head.

"Huh, what you say?" He asked me.

"Oh nothing, Just thinking out loud" I said. How embarrassing was that?

Ryan returned with the bottle of water and handed it to me. As I extended my hand to take the water he pulled me up from the armchair and over to the to the sofa with him. We sat with the TV on but never watched it we just talked about everything under the sun, from what schools we attended to his ex wife and my baby daddy. I kept looking at his eyes, they were seducing me.

"I bet you get all your women with those eyes" I said.

"Nah, I've been married for ten years and never cheated. But you know how people just out grow each other? Well, that is what happened with my ex-wife and I," he explained. "We were young when she got pregnant with our daughter and I wanted to do the right thing."

We just stared at each other, then he leaned in and kissed me. I was caught off guard, but it was sweet. I felt my body get weak. My pussy was popping. The kiss got deeper, to the point where he was on top of me with his hand up my shirt. I didn't even push his hand away. My legs fell open like my pussy was ready. It was working on it's own, as if it was not a part of me. I felt his brick pressed up against my pussy. Before I knew it, my pants were down and his Bee was buzzing around the stalk of my flower. My Calla lily was at full bloom, when his Bee stung me. He bit his bottom lip and whispered "ummm, so wet, this is nice." I was in heaven. The room was spinning and I put my nails so deep in his back to hold on for the ride. He yelled from the pain and pleasure at the same time. He stopped, stood on his feet then pulled me up. We kissed hard. It felt as if our tongues were in a fighting match and before I knew it we were pressed up against the wall, next to the fireplace. He picked me up so my legs could wrap around his waist. We fucked on the wall. I played with his nipples as I wound my hips in a half circle motion, while moving up and down. "Work it" he said. My thighs and part of my ass was wet from all my syrup flowing full force all over his pipe. We both screamed as the pipe broke. It was a flood in that bitch. We hit the floor so hard I jumped. Blinking real fast. What the fuck? I fell off the damn sofa? I was still in my house watching "Brothers." I really need a fucking life.

CHAPTER 6

I got up and went to the bathroom to shake this off. I splashed some water on my face. I think it is time for me to get some help because this is getting out of hand. No one in the world hallucinates this damn much about sex. I went back into the living room and turned on the computer. I googled *sex therapists*. There were so many to choose from. I had no idea where to begin. I found one lady named Lavern Moon. Her office is located here in Richmond. I wrote her number down so I could call her on Monday. I logged off. It was around nine in the evening and the kids had not come home yet. So, I called Sean to see how long they would be.

"We are on the way why? He asked. You sexing right now?" Urgggh, he erks my nerves. It is not all about sex but that is what comes out his mouth every time he talks to me. So got damn annoying. Never responding I just said ok and ended the call.

When they got to the house I was ready for bed. Sean asked if he could come in to talk. I let him in but made his ass stay in the living room while I went to make sure the kids took their showers for the night and went to bed. When I came back in, I sat down next to Sean to see what the hell he wanted. Here he go, "so when you gonna let me hit that? You need it as much as I do and you know it." I think this is all his fault. Every day I talk to him he is asking for some pussy. Since I haven't had dick in like, forever, this shit makes me wonder about every man (or women for that matter) that I see, just so I don't have to fuck him.

Ok this is to all the guys: Just because we have a child together does not mean you will always have access to the pussy. And, women stop upping the cooch when they say "you know I love you." You know damn well they don't love you, they just love 'the good, good' as Ashanti says. Move the hell on.

"I've had it. You need to leave my house, you are very disrespectful and I'm done" I said pushing him away. He jumped up with the screw face and left the house slamming the door behind him. I locked the door and went to bed.

The alarm clock went off. It is now 5:05 AM. Did I just hit the snooze button? Had I imagined the whole thing? Each day? Each episode? Everything? I looked at the clock and it was Thursday. I CAN'T BELIEVE THIS SHIT... I needed to get my ass up and get ready for work. I can't believe I am this damn lonely. I got out of bed went in the bathroom and turned on the shower. I heard buzzing. Is that my cell phone?

"Hello"...

"Good morning Boo," the deep voice on the other line said. "Oh my bad, I forgot, you not my Boo"

"Huh?" WHAT THE HELL.

"Ryan?"

NAKED LADY

mzScorpion

Once upon a time in a far away land, there lived a young, sexy, black princesses who was so beautiful all the knights wanted to marry her. *Laughing my ass off, let me stop.* My name is Mehlika James and my life is far from a fairy tale. It is more like; Who did it and ran? Let me break it down for you. It all started when I was thirteen. That was when I learned the meaning of "ejaculation." I raced home from school wanting to tell my mother all about what I learned in health class but of course she was nowhere to be found. It was normal for her not to be home. I couldn't understand why she was out so much. She didn't have a job, she just liked running the streets I guess. Anyway, my mom's boyfriend lived with us. He was home that day so I asked him if I could talk to him about what I learned in health class. I had more questions. I looked at him like a father figure, until this day. We sat at the kitchen table while I talked.

"How does it work?" I asked. "Pregnancy, you know, what starts the cycle? How come some women get pregnant but some don't? What does X an Y mean?" I was full of questions.

He explained that once a female gets her period, the process begins. That is why condoms are so important.

"If you decide to have sex, you need to make sure to use a condom," he tells me. Then he asked me if I knew how to put one on.

"Heck no I said. I'm a girl, we don't wear condoms. Plus, I'm only thirteen, so why would I know how to put one on?" "You should always know how it works and how to put it on just for your own safety" he said.

"Huh?" My left eyebrow went down and the right one went up as the confusion settled on my face. Just when I was going to ask what he meant, he got up and went to the bedroom. He came back with a condom in hand. "Let me show you" he said. He stood in front of me while leaning against the kitchen counter. He unzipped his pants, removed his penis out through the slit and gripped it real tight, as if he was choking a chicken. He began teasing the head with his thumb while stroking it. I just sat there watching as it increased in size, the head matured with a glossy finish. Once it was standing on its own, he ripped the condom pack open with his teeth and pulled the rubber circle out, then he rolled it over the head and down the shaft. He jerked it over and over again giving himself pleasure. What was I suppose to do? Run? Scream? Yell? Shit, I was young I didn't know what the hell was going on. He closed his eyes allowing his head to slightly fall back. His nostrils flaring in and out like a rhino going in for the kill. A few seconds later white cream escaped the tip of his dick into the tip of the condom. He was panting softly. He slid over to the chair and sat down. As he was removing the condom making sure not to spill any of his juice he said "this is why guys should always wear condoms, because all of this could be up in you and you could get pregnant."

I just sat there with a dumb look on my face, never saying a word. I guess my reaction gave off a welcome mat because every night after that he would sneak in my room slowly sliding his hands under my sheets and fondling my unripe apricot. I was so scared, but never stopped him. Then he started getting bolder. He progressed to using his mouth to taste my sweet spot. I think they call this "eating you out" I remember thinking. I would move him away but he would never stop. I had tried to tell my mother, but she would tell me to stop making up lies. Then, one day I was awakened by what felt like heavy breathing in my face. I opened my eyes and there he was, hovered over me. In between my legs I could feel pressure at the tip of my Vagina. He was pushing harder. I began to cry and tried to push him off. He was like dead weight. There was no moving him. I raised my knee, making sure it connected to his groin and it was over. I could not begin to fathom what was going through this man's head. I was only a pre-teenager and was like a daughter to him. If this is what a father does with his daughter, then I don't want any girls. I cried every night after that afraid to sleep alone.

Several years passed and I was now attending college and living on my own. I never brought up what happened to me with my stepfather to anyone, I just moved on. I was living in the Bronx on 151st street and the

Grand Concourse, right above the Amtrak rail road tracks which was cool because I loved sitting on my fire escape at night reading a good book just watching the trains go by. But, here is when my other problems started.

One day, one of my good friends, boyfriend approached me in the break room and asked if I could help him write a paper for German studies. Since I was on the tutoring roster, I said sure we can meet in the library at 6 pm. When 6 pm hit he was walking through the door. I loved tutoring during that time because the amount of people in the library was pretty much next to none, so I thought it would be the perfect time to help him with no distractions. I had already pulled a few books out for research and placed them on the table. He sat down, pulled out his note pad and we got started. At one point we got stuck and needed more information, so I got up to look for another book and he came along with me. We were standing way in the back of the library between the bookshelves, when he leaned in and kissed me.

"Wait hold up…NO" I said pushing him back. "What are you doing?" He said "C'mon you know you want it. I saw how you kept looking at me, acting like you had to come get another book. You need to stop playing games and just say you want me to hit it." Then he pushed me up on the shelf and placed his hand over my mouth to keep me quiet. He unzipped his pants pulled his dick out while pulling my skirt up. This bastard was really going to have sex with me forcefully. I was having flashbacks from those times with my stepfather. My eyes just welled with tears as I slowly closed them, tight. I knew I could not stop him. He fucked me so hard I was bleeding and no one was there to help. It always seems that way. No one is ever around for proof.

When he was done I collapsed on the floor and cried. He zipped his pants and left like nothing happened. What the fuck is wrong with men? I just don't get it. Why do they think it is ok to take the pussy whenever they want, from whomever they want? I refused to go back to school after that incident. I was depressed to the point that I started thinking about killing myself. I actually laid in my tub with a box cutter ready to take my life. Just then my phone rang; I got out the tub to answer it.

"Hello…"

"Hey ma'ma, what'cha doing? I haven't seen you in school for a couple of days and you haven't even called me. What's going on?" "It's me, Leche," the voice on the other end said.

"I'm fine, just tired" I replied.

"Well Im'a come by to check on you and make sure you are eating" she said.

"Ok sure, that will be fine."

Leche is my best friend and the craziest Puerto Rican you would ever meet. I love her to death. We hung up the phone and went back to the bathroom and let the water out of the tub. I took a quick shower instead. I put on some sweat pants and a tee shirt, pulled my hair back in a pony tail and walked in the kitchen. I jumped when the buzzer from the doorbell went off. It scared the crap out of me. I pressed the intercom

"Yes?"

"It's me chica… Leche."

Wow that was fast. She must have already been in my neighborhood when she called to check on me. "Ok come on up." I buzzed her in, unlocked the door and sat on the couch. A few minutes later Leche was coming through the door.

"Hey ma'ma" she smiled as she closed and locked the door behind her. "These are for you."

She handed me a plant with the most beautiful purple flowers. We hugged. God I love her. She always knows how to make me feel better.

"They are called "Autumn Crocus," we studied and dissected these plants in my biology class," Leche said as she looked around the room. "I knew you would like it since your favorite color is purple, so I picked one up for you. I got them from the fruit stand on my block."

"They are beautiful, I love them. Thank you chica" I said as I placed them on my TV mantel and gave her another big hug. "You are the best" I told her.

We sat down on the sofa and started talking. She asked what's been going on with me and why have you been MIA? I told her I just hadn't been feeling so well and needed some time to myself.

"Is everything ok with school? Are you coming back? Talk to me!" She sounded concerned.

I said yeah, it's all good and that I would be back on that Monday. We ordered pizza and watched movies while we played catch up. Leche was telling me about how she told her parents she was gay and how they reacted. They made her leave the house and told her never to come back. She has shamed her family. I felt so bad, but she said she was fine with it. She had moved in with her girlfriend and her roommate.

"Don't let those Bitches fuck you over or treat you any kind'a way, I don't wanna have to hurt nobody" I told her banging my right fist in my left hand gesturing like I was beating on someone. We busted out laughing.

Time was flying and before we knew it, it was ten o'clock. Leche had to leave. She had to go to work in the morning. She got her things together and I walked her to the door.

"I will see you Monday in calc class right?" She asked me.

"Yep, make sure you call me when you get home." We hugged then I closed and locked the door. I cleaned up the living room, put the leftover pizza away and went to turn off the TV when I noticed the plant. What kind of plant did she say this was? I turned on my laptop went to Google. I typed in the name *Autumn Crocus*. The information for proper care popped up first. All it needed was a little water every other day and to make sure and keep it in a dark warm area. Then I noticed the plant had a very intriguing name, "The Naked Lady." The name comes from the fact that It blossoms because of death. Just like me. I've been scorned but you would never know it because I appear so delicate and lovely on the outside. But you don't want to know what may be hiding on the inside. This plant and I are a perfect match. I turned off the computer and went to bed.

CHAPTER 2

As promised, I went back to school the following Monday. But I had only one thing on my mind... PAY BACK! Days had gone by and I hadn't seen dude anywhere. I was burning with fire to put him on blast but never had the chance. Instead other dudes were asking me out. Now, these guys never talked to me before and they all have girlfriends. I bet dude told them I give up the cooch real easy. So they figured they will get some ass too. Ok, I got you. I went on a few dates just to ease my mind. After each date I would call Leche to tell her who I was with and where we went, you know, all the details. Leche thought I was crazy. "You are way to pretty to be wasting your time with these guys? Fuck them!" She would always say. Hahaha I do fuck'em. Shit, I gott'a get something out of it. She hated the fact that I was lowering myself to those standards.

It was Saturday morning and I stepped out to grab some breakfast. I walked to my favorite eatery at the corner of 149th street and Grand Concourse. Yummy Tummies Diner had the best French toast ever. "Hey you, I thought you were going to call me back with a date for us to catch a flick what's up?" a voice said from behind. I jumped and turned around real quick to see who was talking to me. Calvin Thomas, the cutie with the goatee from my office technology class. He was my partner last week for a job interview project. I agreed to go out to the movies with him if we got an A. He was one of the basketball players at our school and was going out with this girl Nina. Nina is a real nice girl and we all know she is sooo in love with Calvin but as you see he don't give two shits about her.

"Hey you," I replied. "I didn't even see you there", I continued as I let the door handle go and the door closed slowly. I folded my arms across my chest. "I know, I didn't forget. I've just been busy. But I'm free tonight, how about you?" He was mad hyped when I said tonight.

"Yeah, yeah, tonight is real good. What is your address so I can pick you up?" he asked.

"Naw… I don't want you to pick me up I will meet you there. What time is good?" I asked.

"The movie I want to see starts at 9:15, so can you meet me like at 8:30?" I flashed him a big smile and said

"see you then."

I opened the door, went inside and sat at the counter.

Breakfast was delicious and now I needed a nap. I walked two blocks back to my apartment. As soon as I walked through the door I put my bag down on the couch and pressed the answering machine to check my messages. I had two but they were from Leche wanting me to call her back ASAP. I went in the bedroom and opened the closet. Uhmm what should I wear, I thought. Since it was just the movies, I figured I didn't have to put on anything to sexy. I pulled out a pair of black skinny leg jeans, a black tee with purple writing and placed them on my bed. I called Leche back to see what was going on.

"Yo what up chica?" I said when she answered.

"Nothing what are you doing today, I'm bored."

I told her I'd just gotten back from Yummy Tummies and bout to study for this final for Tuesday.

"Damn you always got your head in the books, I wanted to hang out or something" she whined.

"My bad, but I need to get an A in this class then I would make the President's list. Plus, I'm going out tonight with Calvin Thomas."

"Scratch that" she said. "You always got your legs spread open, you stay getting fucked."

"Wow I can't believe you just said that to me. That was fucked up. Look I got to go." I hung up.

I gathered my books and sat on my bed. For the next six hours I was hitting the books hard. It was 4:00PM and my stomach had sunk to my back. I was starving. I made me two hot dogs and watched TV. Before I knew it, it was 6:30 and I needed to get ready for my date. I went to the bathroom and started the shower when I heard the phone ringing. I bet its Leche… I'll call her later. I closed the bathroom door, put my shower cap on and stepped in the hot steamy water. I used my "At First Sight" body scrub from Victoria's Secret to make sure my pussy was giving off the right "come and get it" scent. I finished my shower and went in the bedroom, sat on the bed and applied my body lotion all over. Once dressed, I stood in front of the mirror on my dresser combing my hair down, but making sure to keep the curls intact. I like the full body look. I winked to myself, sexy ass!

I left my apartment and headed to the train station. Half way to the corner of my block a black expedition pulled up next to me. A voice from inside the truck said "excuse me are you Mehlika James?" *Word to the wise, when a car, truck, SUV or any moving vehicle pulls up next to you and someone ask you if you are you... Bitch RUN, cause it can't be good.* But they were too close for me to do that. "Who's asking?" I said in a boorish tone. The driver put the truck in park and the guy who was asking got out from the passenger side, holding a badge.

"May I have a moment of your time?" he asked.

"Just one moment, because I have some where to be," I said as he approached me.

"We just have a few questions for you," he said as he pulled out a small black note pad and flipped it open. He quickly began his questioning.

"Do you know somcone by the name of Peter Green?"

"Yeah, I went out on a date with him a few days ago but, haven't heard from him since, why?" I asked.

"Where did you meet him?"

"In school, he asked me out I said yes. Why are you here" I asked.

"He was found dead in his apartment by his girl friend and we have reason to believe he was murdered. We are investigating the case and need to speak with anyone who may have been in contact with him prior to his death...your number was the last one he called" the detective said.

I said, "ok but I can't help you, I told you we went on a date a few days ago and again I haven't heard from him since. But now I see why. I have to go."

I walked off and headed to the train station.

I met Calvin in front of the theater. He kissed me on my cheek and we went inside. He was all over me as we watched the movie. "I want you so bad" he said while licking my earlobe. I leaned closer to him moving my hand slowly down his crouch so I could caress his penis. "Ooooh, yeah that's right girl you know what I like." I unzipped his jeans and pulled his dick out so I could get a better grip. He must have washed right before he met up with me cause I could smell the Axe Body Wash scent rising. I turned his face towards mine and asked him would you like me right now.

He drew in air, "yes girl come get it." He was ready. I took his drink out of his hand and placed it in his side cup holder and pulled a condom out my purse. I ripped it open with my teeth and rolled it over the head then down the shaft of his dick. I made it a point to pull the tip up some to make sure there was space for his semen. No popping on my watch. I pulled my jeans down and removed one leg. Slowly, I descended on his dick. I faced the screen so it was not obvious I was riding him. Calvin grabbed my ass like it was a basketball and he was bouncing it on the court. I moved in slow motion giving him what he wanted. I was like a cat in the night, smooth, soft, quite and flexible pouncing on my prey. His body tensed up underneath me making me aware of his eruption but I was not ready so before he could cum I stopped, turned my body around to face him and got back on top. I pulled my right breast out and shoved it in his mouth to hush him up, just like you with do a baby to stop them from crying. Then I alternated my hips making sure we were in sync. Calvin's teeth bit down on the tip of my nipple making me extremely aware of the feeling. He couldn't hold back anymore. It was time to bust that nut. His body tweaked a few times under me then I got up and sat in the seat next to him.

"Girl you are off the chain… DAMN" he said in short breaths. I smiled and said "I'm glad you liked it." I handed him some napkins so he could remove the condom and wipe himself off. He was out of breath. He cleaned off and put his shit away then picked up his drink. He drank gulp after gulp, trying to catch his breath. "You wore me out" he said between swallows. "Naw, you good Hon, we just having fun right?" I asked. "Yeah that was fun, you are the best." He drank the rest of his soda and leaned back to watch the movie, but more so to enjoy his lay. I got up and he asked me where I was going. I grabbed my purse, pulled out a small purple flower and said I was going to the restroom to clean up. "I'll be right back." I handed him the flower and walked out of the theater.

Once outside, I went up to one of the taxis parked out front and got in the back seat. "Take me to 151st and Grand Concourse" I ordered the cabby. I pulled out my cell phone to check if I had missed any calls. The first one was from Leche. "Hey chica, just calling to see what you were up to, hoping you didn't go on that damn date and you just mad at me for keeping it real. Give me a call later ok love you mi amor." The second call was from Lamar, he and I have plans to meet up tomorrow night. "Good evening miss lady. Just touching base with you for tomorrow. Are we still on? Hit me up boo." I closed my phone and rolled my eyes in disgust. I called Leche back.

"Haylo" she answered.

"Hey gurl, where you at?" I asked.

"I'm home where are you?" I told her I had just finished my date and was on my way home.

"Were you trying to get up?" I asked.

"Well I was gonna stop by and give you the update on my situation but not sure if you want me around and all since you hung up on me earlier," Leche said.

"Cauz you said some fucked up shit, but it's all good. I know you love me, so sure I will be home in like twenty minutes, if you get there before me just use your key to get in" I told her.

"Ok cool" she said and asked me if she could stay over that night. I said sure no problem and told her I would see her in a few. I put my cell back in my purse and looked out the window for the rest of the ride, watching the scenery as we drove through the Bronx. It is such a shame to see people standing around not doing anything with their lives.

When we approached my building the driver stopped right in front. I pulled out a twenty and passed it to him through the half-window. He gave me back seven bucks and I got out. When I got to my apartment Leche was already inside. She opened the door as I approached. She said she heard me in the hallway.

"Hey, how long you been here?" I asked. She said she had just gotten there.

"You hungry?" she asked me. I said sure, let me go wash up first. While I took my shower Leche was preparing frozen Tyson's chicken nuggets and Orida fries. We climbed in my bed with our plates and watched The Color "Purple. She told me how her girlfriend and roommate get high all day long, don't clean, and eat every fucking thing she buys.

"Tell dem bitches to get a job and help you out" I told her.

"I would, she said, but they'd just look at me like I'm speaking another language."

"Shit, you do!" We started laughing. "But on the real, sit your girl down and let her know how you feel and if she don't change you will leave" I said.

"Yeah im'a try dat tomorrow" Leche sighed.

We dogged our food, put the plates in the kitchen and finished watching The Color Purple until we fell asleep.

CHAPTER 3

In the morning Leche took a shower while I used the toilet. She was fussing about being late for work. "Well if you hurry the hell up we both can get out of here on time, I do have to wash my body too" I yelled over the loud, splashing water hitting the porcelain shower. I wiped but did not flush because it makes the water cold in the shower. "Wait, leave the water running" I said as she stepped out of the shower. I stepped in. We continued our conversation with me yelling over the shower while she was getting ready. We left together but headed in different directions. "I will see you later, I said. Have a good day at work."

I ran upstairs to the subway platform to catch my train. I was headed to school but decided to stop at Leche's place and have a talk with her peoples. I knocked on the door and Ja'nell, the roommate, answered in her boxers and a wife beater. "Come In Mehlika, what can we do for you. You know Leche is not here right?" she said as we walked back into the living room.

"I know, I'm here to talk to ya'll" I replied. Leche's girlfriend Mona came in the living room where we were now sitting. The apartment reeked of weed and you can tell they were bent the hell up. I just broke it down,

"you two are so fucked up sitting around here getting high, not paying bills, eating everything my home girl buys and not helping her out. Then you two got the nerve to laugh in her face?" They both began to cop a plea, Ja'nell starts with

"she always be in here talking down to us like we her kids." Mona adds how Leche is always being cheap with the pussy, "I have needs just like the next chick." She sat on the sofa in front of me with her legs gapped open showing off a clean shaved cat. Then Ja'nell, who was sitting next to me looked me right in the eyes and said

"we can hook you up… if you like."

"Huhhh?" what you mean hook me up? I don't smoke weed or anything else" I quickly confessed.

"I was talking about showing you what we do to help each other out round here" Ja'nell said in a sexy voice as she moved closer to me, taking her index finger and tracing the side of my neck while licking her lips. Mona slid off the sofa until she was face-to-face with my crouch. She unbuttoned my jeans and began slowly pulling my zipper down. Ja'nell took her hand sliding up my shirt cupping my breast whispering in my ear, "just relax." I was so confused about what was going on but my pussy was getting moist. Mona grabbed the sides of my jeans tugging and pulling them down revealing my boy shorts. Ja'nell's kissing me on my neck was making me so hot. How they managed to have me laying on my back on the sofa without me realizing it, I could not tell you. Ja'nell straddled my face making her pussy place soft kisses on my lips leaving wet spots each time she came down. Mona took off my underwear and pushed my legs apart so she could lick my muff. She slid the hood of my clit back with her thumb, while her tongue massaged it. My pussy was making all kinds of smacking noises and between the two of them my ass was going bananas. Ja'nell directed me to stick my tongue in and out of her hole and nibble on her clit. I obeyed each command and she held the top of my head and wined her hips smashing her pussy on my face. I was climbing the walls. A man had never made me feel what I was feeling at that moment. I was really missing out.

We went at it for about an hour switching positions giving each other organisms. By the time it was over, the three of us was laying on the living room floor, butt ass naked. I glanced at the clock on the cable box and it read 11:23AM. "Oh shit I have to go" I said as I jumped up grabbing my clothes. I was all tripping over the girls trying to get my legs in my pants. I ran in the bathroom to finish getting dressed, thinking what the HELL did I just do? I fucked my best friends girlfriend AND her girlfriend's best friend. Damn! If Leche knew this shit she would hate me for the rest of my life. I left the apartment without saying a word to those bitches. They set me up. I just told myself it never happened as I headed to school so I could finish my report. I was sitting in study hall when I felt a light tap on my shoulder. I turned to see Lamar standing over me. "Can I sit here?"

he asked wondering if the seat next to me was taken. What a fiend. "Sure sit, I said, what's up?"

"You tell me shawty. Are we still good for tonight?" he asked.

"Oh yeah, I can't wait" I said sounding like a little kid running for the ice-cream truck. "What is the name of the restaurant again?" I asked. He said it was called "Billie's Black Bar and Lounge" on west 119th street and Frederick Douglas.

"It sounded like an upscale place so I figured you would like that," he said. I smiled and told him

"yes that sounds real nice." I told him I would prefer to meet you there since it was not far from my place.

He said "fine, but the place closes at midnight tonight so I will meet you at 8 o'clock agreed?"

"Yes"

"OK cool, see you later" he said, then he walked off.

I completed my assignment then headed over to the staff desk to check what time my next student would be in for their tutoring session. Maybe I had some time to grab a bite to eat. Mr. Legamin handed me the folder for the next student and grazed my wrist giving me a seductive look. "I can be your next student if you want Mehlika," he said and laughed. He was always in my damn face with his old ass. His breath smelling like hot horse shit. I snatched the folder telling him he is silly and walked off. His fugly ass made me shiver. I opened the folder to see who was on the list. Name: Danielle Longmier. Time: 3:00 pm. I didn't have to meet the chic until three, so I'm gonna go get me some grub. I left the building and walked to the corner. I chose Taco Bell. While checking the menu I noticed these two dudes peeping me from the sideline. I ordered two soft beef tacos, a medium Pepsi and a chocolate chip cookie. I took my order and walked out. I was headed back to the school when I heard my name being called from behind. I turned and it was the two dudes from Taco Bell.

"Yes can I help you?" I said.

"Do you remember me from last night?" It was the undercover detective that was asking me about Peter.

"Yeah I think you asked me some questions about my friend Peter right?"

"Yes, yes I did, well I need to ask you some more questions. This time it's about a gentlemen by the name Calvin Thomas and a few other gentlemen" he said.

"Well, give me your card and I will give you a call when I have the time but right now I have something important to do" I said, extending my hand. The detective was persistent.

"This will just take a minute." Can he not hear?

"Again, I have something to do, so if you don't have a card then I can't help you."

He stuck his hand inside his jacket, pulled out some business cards and handed me one.

"Call me when you have time Ms. James" he said. His partner never said a word.

"Sure no problem." They walked off and I went back in the school.

I met up with Danielle in the cafeteria. She had just sat down with her lunch so I joined her. She pulled out all of her notes and we got started. We worked from 3:00 to 5:00. When we finished studying, she signed her name on the form and left. I took the form to the front office to turn it in and headed home so I can relax before my date tonight with Lamar. When I got home I gave my little plant some water. I went into the bedroom, took off my clothes and laid across the bed. I turned on the TV and before I knew it I had dozed off. I was woken up out our my sleep by loud knocking. I could hear my neighbor yelling "let me in you know I lost my keys". She was always getting locked out of her apartment. Dumb ass! As she continued to knock on her door I rolled out my bed and headed to the bathroom. It was 6:45 and I needed to get ready. I jumped in the shower making sure to wash every inch of my body. Got out, dried off and walked back into the bedroom. I opened my closet and pulled out a short, fitted metallic gold dress from Baby Phat the "Bejeweled Collection." I ordered it from the website. I paired it with the "Porsha's" also by Baby Phat. I rubbed myself down with lotion then got dressed. I put soft drop curls in my hair and swooped the front. I added a touch of eyeliner to my eyes to bring out the shape and color. I grabbed my gold clutch, checked the mirror one last time and was out the door. I arrived right on time. Lamar had just walked in to get a table when I pulled up. I went inside to meet him. "You look sexy as hell," he said, giving me a peck on the cheek. The waiter seated us and took our drink order. I ordered an Apple Martini and he got a Mojito. I pushed his drink to the side so I can hold his hand and talk before dinner.

The food was real good and the atmosphere made me hot. We talked about school and what celebrity we would marry. We had such a good time but I was ready for some dick action. We hailed a cab and headed to his place. I caressed his dick through his jeans to wake it up. I love when it is all ready for me. We reached his place and fondled each other all the way into the house. Removing each other's clothes tripping over furniture and falling back onto the sofa. Lamar bent down and removed my thongs with his teeth, flinging them off to the side somewhere. It was too dark for me to see where they landed. His lips were soft and warm as they massaged my moist spot. I spread my wings, ready to fly. His thick wet tongue began to dip deep into my pussy, pulling out pre cum. The heat was rising from the core of my body making me so sultry. I grabbed his head holding it in place so he can hit my spot real good. When I cum I like it to be real hard, making it well worth the fuck. I held his head, and raised my hips to get into the motion. He knew just what to do, flicking his tongue against the tip of my clit. It was driving me crazy. I yelled "yes daddy get it get it" as I rocked my hips making sure I felt each vibration. Oh yeah I was cumming just like I like.

I pushed him back so I could get up. I turned around getting on all fours hiking my ass in the air. Lamar stood behind me ready to enter. I reached around and spread my ass and pussy open so he can get a good view of the pink stuff. "Damn you a undercover freak" Lamar said as he straddled me like we were two dogs in the woods. He placed one leg on the sofa next to me and the other was on the floor. I felt his hands grab my waist and just like that, BAM, he was in me like he never had pussy before. I bounced back on his dick while arching my back allowing him to go deeper. Before I knew it he was calling my name. He was digging his nails into my hips and biting his bottom lip trying to gain control and his balance as he erupted into flames. My work here was done.

He fell over on the floor and I sat down on the sofa, both of us breathing heavily. After a few seconds I told him I had to go because I had to get up early. He just sat on the floor and said "Ok. Give me a call tomorrow."

"I sure will. But until then… think of me" as I tossed a small purple flower on his lap. I pulled my dress down, slipped my purse under my arm and walked out. When I got outside I walked to the corner and entered the subway heading uptown. Shit, I left my underwear, I thought while standing on the platform awaiting my train. When I got home I took a nice long, hot shower but this time I went to bed in my birthday suit. I got in the bed picked up the phone and checked my messages. Wow! No messages, what a shocker and a relief. I needed a break from all this sexing. I turned the TV on and the show "Friends" was on. That was my favorite show. I watched it and laughed until I fell asleep.

CHAPTER 4

The next morning my I-pod was playing "Rock The Boat" by Aaliyah while I stretched, doing palates. I think it is good to be very flexible if you are gonna be putting your business down. My phone rang. I answered

"Hello."

"Hey girl, are you working out right now?" It was Leche.

"Yeah why, what'z up?"

"I knew it. You are so predictable," Leche said as she chuckled into the phone. " Anyway I want you to go to the mall with me."

"What time were you planning on going?" I asked

"Like now, that is why I'm calling… HELLLOOO"

"Don't get smart," I said, and we both laughed. I told her sure and to come on over while I got ready. I hung up the phone, did my last five minutes of stretches then jumped in the shower. I turned the showerhead on full force and the way it hit my body sent me over the edge. I pulled it down so I could hold it right in front of my vagina. The water did a tap dance all over me. I closed my eyes, imagining I was getting my shit ate the fuck out. I was just about to reach my explosion when I heard "Mehlika I'm here" Got damn it. "I'll be right out" I yelled from the bathroom. I had to finish so I would not have a knot in my stomach. If I don't bust, that shit hurt like hell. I released my nut, washed my pussy and got out of the shower. That nut was not good because I was interrupted but it will have to do. I walked back into my room and sat on the bed to lotion up when Leche walked in.

"Hey. Hurry up I need to get my eyebrows done and you know I like to go before it get crowed" she said, rushing me. "Ok, ok you see I'm getting ready. What else you going to get from the mall?" I asked.

"I don't know, I just needed to get out that damn house, those bitches are getting on my fucking nerves" Leche complained. I busted out laughing

"You stupid. I told you to talk to your girl" I said, feeling a little guilty. She gave me a funny look and I just put my head down.

"I know but I want to hang out with my best friend today. Cool?" She asked.

"Cool," I replied.

I got dressed and we headed out the door. We went to Fulton street mall in downtown, Brooklyn. Leche stopped in one of the nail salons that do eyebrow threading. I've gotta admit, threading always looks hot, way better then waxing. I told the lady I wanted mine done too. This will be my first time, but I so needed them done. I sat in a chair by the window and watched the people shop. I saw two females walking around with fake Gucci bags and Dolce and Gabbana shades, as if they were on Rodeo Drive. They just knew they were the shit. People are too funny. After we were done with our eyebrows, we went to Tony's famous pizza shop to have lunch, then walked around catching up on gossip and checking out the goods. You know, the hood dudes, for me, of course. Anyway, we bought a few things then walked to Juniors for the best cheesecake ever. It was getting late and I was ready to go home. We headed over to Nevins street train station to catch the 2 train, uptown. I reached in my purse to get my metro card and pulled out the card from the detective instead. Drawing my teeth in, making a sucking sound, I flicked the card on the ground and reached back in my purse to get my metro card. Leche was already standing on the platform asking me what I was doing. I slid my card through the turn style and went through, "nothing" I assured her. I got off at 149th and Grand Concourse but Leche stayed on the train and kept going. She had to go to 171st. I reached my building and noticed that black expedition was right in front. I walked over to the truck and they rolled the windows down.

"Hi there, Ms. James" the detective said as he opened the front passenger door of the truck and got out. "May I have a moment of your time?"

"Are you spying on me detective?" I said with a smirk. He smiled.

"No, no, I just stopped by so I can ask you a few questions Ms. James. Is that okay?"

I said "okay," and told him he could come upstairs for a few, but it was late, so make it short. He signaled his partner and he got out of the truck. He locked the doors and we all headed up to my apartment.

As we entered the apartment, I pointed to the left towards the living room. "We can talk in here" I said. "So how can I help you detectives?" I sat my bags down next to the entertainment unit and directed my attention to the two police officers now standing in the middle of my living room.

"I'm detective Roice and this is my partner detective Johns" the one that gave me his card said. "So when was the last time you saw Calvin Thomas?" Wow, straight to the point.

"The night we went out on a date why?" I answered abruptly.

"Well Ms. James, he was found dead, just like Peter Green was found dead. Right after they each went on a date with you. And there are other gentlemen we believe you had last contact with before they too were found dead," detective Roice said

"Ok first, I never killed anyone and who are these other gentlemen you keep referring to?" I asked. Detective Roice pulled out his little black pad, flipped it open and read some names.

"Evan Nicholas, Chris Christopher, Dylan Carter, and the last one found last night Lamar Washington."

"So you saying I murdered these men? And how did they die? Because, that just seems so strange to me that a small female like me can brutally murder some big ass men" I said, calmly.

"They were not brutally murdered," He said. "More like poisoned." I had a look on my face of complete and utter shock.

"Poisoned? I'm not sure if I understand what you are saying. How could they have been poisoned? And, are you sure?" I asked. The detective assured me he was sure. He said each of them died the same way; fever, vomiting, diarrhea, than sever pain sending them into hypovolemic shock.

"We just don't know what caused the reaction and was hoping you could help us since you were the last person they were with" he explained. I told him I wasn't sure how I could be of any assistance.

"I mean I did go out on a date with each of them but they took me to different places so, it couldn't have been the food. And I know I ain't sick so I don't understand," I explained to the detectives.

Detective Johns was looking at the pictures on top of my entertainment unit and smelling my flowers.

"These are very pretty Ms. James," he said. "What are they?"

"They are called Autumn Crocus. They only grow from the ground in dark, cold places long after the leaves have died" I answered.

I told him it had been a gift from my best friend and asked him not to touch it. Detective Roice said

"Ok Ms. James, I see we've taken up enough of your time. If we have any further questions can we give you a call?" I said sure and gave him my cell number. He wrote it in his black note pad then they headed out the door. I locked the door behind them and went in the kitchen to pour me a glass of Pepsi. I removed my clothes, climbed into bed and turned on the TV. I was watching the news when:

"News at 11... Another man found dead in his apartment making this a total of six men. Investigators are saying these men all died from arsenic poising. Police are looking at a few possible suspects. Stay tuned for further updates."

Look at this shit. I could not believe it. This was some crazy shit. I laid my head on the pillow and tried to sleep.

CHAPTER 5

"Good morning Mr. Legamin. How are you," I asked, as I entered the Library. "I'm doing just fine now that I see you Mehlika," he replied in his regular nasty way. Urggh, he is just disgusting. I don't want his nasty old wrinkled ass. I just gave him a smirk and kept it moving. I walked to the back where the computers were and logged on. I wanted to check my emails from school to see who signed up for tutoring. Just then my cell phone starts vibrating. It was an unknown number.

"Speak to me" I said.

"Hi, Mrs. James… this is detective Roice. Did I catch you at a bad time?"

"Yeah you did, I'm in school. How can I help you?" He was getting on my last nerve.

"I was wondering if you would like to have dinner with me tonight?"

"Ummm, detective, aren't you married? I know I saw a wedding band," I said, in a confused voice.

"Yes I am, but this is business. What do you say?" He insisted. These motherfuckers are a trip. There was a silent pause before I answered. I took a deep breath and let out a big sigh,

"Where we going?" I asked.

"BBQ's in Washington Heights, located on the corner of 166th and Broadway," he answered, quickly. I love that place. "Sure what time" I asked.

"How does seven o'clock sound?"

I said cool and told him to make sure he made reservations because that place is always packed. We said bye and hung up. I reviewed my emails and noticed I had four people signed up for tutoring that day. I called them all back to give them times and places to meet. It was almost 10 am so I figured each one would study with me for two hours, that way I could be done by 5:00PM. That would leave plenty of time to get ready for my date... with detective Roice. Huh! I called Leche to tell her what was going on but she did not answer her phone so I left her a message. "Hey love I am going on a date tonight with the detective I told you about, we are going to BBQ's on 166th. Ok hit me up before seven, bye." As I walked out the library I noticed a memorial banner for the guys from the school that died, so I signed my name paying my respects, then headed out to meet my first student.

5:00 rolled around so fast. I was all done with my tutoring sessions and was about to head home. I was contemplating what I was going to wear when my cell chimed. I had a message. It was a text from DT Roice... *C U soon (smiley face.)* I didn't even respond. He was too happy to be going out with me. I laughed to myself as I watched the New York crazies board the same train I was getting on. I reached my stop and got off making my way to my building. I was ready for some leave me the fuck alone sex. I took my shower as usual, lotion myself down with the come get it cream. I was ready.

I put on some boot cut jeans, my blue, white and sliver wedges and a blue tee that look like someone splashed white paint all over it with the words "ROCKER" written in sliver. I grabbed my small silver handbag and walked out the door. BBQ's was not too far from my place, so there was no need to take the train or hail a cab. I just took the bus. Right before my stop I stood up, applied some more lip-gloss and walked to the back door. I hit the rubber strip for the bus to stop at the next stop and let me off. I could see detective Roice as the bus approached the stop. He looked like the artist, Mario Barrett, he was fine. Now how the HELL did I not notice this before? I don't know. I waved as I got off the bus and walked over to him. He kissed me on the cheek.

"You look nice," I said, as we entered the restaurant.

"Well thank you. And just to let you know, please call me Curtis."

I just smiled. The host told us to follow him. He placed us at a table that was next to a window facing the hospital, but in a corner away from everyone.

"I'm starving," I said as we sat down.

"Your server will be right with you" the host announced then he walked away. A few seconds later, a big breasted chic walks over to our table

"Good evening guys, my name is Simone and I'll be taking care of you tonight. Let's start with a drink," she said. Her voice was breathy and unusually heavy for a woman. Curtis responded first,

"I'll have a bloody murder." I twisted my face thinking what kind of drink is that? I told the girl I will have an Apple Martini. She said "thanks I'll be right back with your drinks" and walked away. She returned very quickly with the drinks and took our food orders. I got the baked, half-chicken special and he got the crispy shrimp special. While we were sipping our drinks Curtis tells me that the poison found in the men was called Colchicines. It is like arsenic poisoning. It was used to treat gout, but is not FDA approved, so it is not even found in our country. And since none of the guys that had died from this poison were majoring in medicine, he could not figure out where or how they got it until he looked it up on-line and found that Colchicines is from a plant called "Meadow Saffron" also known as "Autumn Crocus" That was the same flower found with each of the bodies. He continued to say he thought maybe they all knew each other and some kind of way bought the flower for their girlfriends. But then he noticed that I had the same Meadow Saffron plant in my apartment.

"So what are you trying to say Curtis?" I asked.

"Why'd you do it?" He said flat out.

"Why'd I do what? I had nothing to do with the murders of those guys. I just went out with them and yes, I fucked them like we were wild baboons but that is all," I said, sipping my martini.

"I am requesting for you to come by the station and supply use with your DNA," Detective Curtis Roice said. "We found a pair of underwear at Lamar Washington's place and since his girlfriend has never seen them before we need you to help us out." I looked him right in his eyes and said,

"you don't need my DNA for that, because if they were a black thong, size 5 from Victoria's Secret, then they are mine...I left them there" He paused.

"Well, I know you have something to do with this, and not just the underwear. And I promise you I, will find out. But until then let's have a good evening." I was at breaking point. He was definitely pissing me off and I was ready to leave. But not before I got some dick. I winked at him and said,

"I think I've had more than enough to drink. can you help me to the bathroom?" I stood up and he got up taking my hand as we walked. He yanked his hand away and told me to go ahead. He went back to the table because I had forgotten my pocket book and he went to get it for me. He walked a few steps back to the table, placed a five dollar tip under the salt shaker and picked up our drinks. Then, he followed me. We went down the steps to the bathroom and I pulled him in and locked the door. He placed the drinks and my purse on the sink and I unbutton his pants, searching for the slit to his boxers so I can devourer him and since we hadn't eaten yet I was hungry. I slobbed his knob like it was nobody's business. I had him up against the sink praying for mercy. I twirled my tongue around the head and down the shaft. I pretended it was a rocket pop. Just when he was ready to bust I pulled back telling him to wait. I pulled down my jeans and bent over touching my toes in front of him. I took my left hand to guide his "magic stick" *as Fifty Cent say* into my pussy. He tells me it is like warm apple pie. "Well let's make some apple juice come out of it," I said. I just held my ankles and backed that thang up. He fondled my pea while dipping in the pot. I let go one of my ankles and reached between my legs and massaged his dumplings. We were both at total explosion. I love when that happens. Bathroom sex is the bomb.

I got my bearings and stood up. He picked up his drink and took a few sips. I walked in the toilet stall so I could pee. I was pulling my pants up when he said just because you rocked my world doesn't mean my case is closed. I flushed the toilet, walked over to the sink and pushed him aside so I could look in the mirror. He handed me my drink. I finished it and sat the glass down. I pulled out my lip-gloss and glided some on. I fixed my hair, adjusted my shirt and handed him a purple flower. I Kissed him on the cheek and whispered in his ear *"say Hi to the Naked Lady."* He handed it back to me, "no love, you need it more than me." I opened the bathroom door and walked out. He never followed me. I hailed a cab and went home. I took a nice hot shower and sang to myself. There is nothing like being alone to study your thoughts. When I got out, I poured me an ice-cold glass of Pepsi and called Leche to see if she wanted to go to the movies tomorrow evening. She told me she found out some real fucked up shit and wasn't sure how to handle it. We talked for the rest of the night.

The next morning Leche was on the phone crying, screaming please help me! Please!

"Maam, what is the emergency?" The 911 operator requested. "Please send an ambulance quick" Leche screamed. The TV in the background told the story...

Breaking News... "Monroe College student, Mehlika James, was found dead in her apartment this morning. A statement from Detective Roice says

56

[Mehlika James was suspected in the Monroe College student murders. 6 men were found dead, each poised after going on a date with Ms. James. It is alleged that she used a rare plant called Autumn Crocus, also known as "The Naked Lady to poison her victims." A search of Ms. James apartment revealed that she had the same plant in her home, which linked her to the murders." More on this story right after these messages...

Leche was heartbroken. She could not believe what she was hearing. The same plant she gave to me, because I loved the color purple, enabled me to commit an unthinkable crime and maybe the very cause of my own death. Now the question is... Who killed Me?

CHELSEA'S WET DREAM

Lynx

I imagined us on a sandy white beach. He had on some linen cargo shorts, and I had on a black sheer cover-up bikini showing off the recent tattoo on my back. We sat on the lounge chairs enjoying a wonderful conversation watching the moonlight cast a walkway to heaven on the ocean as the tide rolled in over the sand.

Deciding to take a walk, we strolled hand in hand. He was making me laugh when out of the blue he stops talking and grabs me close. Looking deep into my eyes he tells me how beautiful I am. I blush not knowing what to say. My heart is beating so fast it feels like it will bust out of my chest. He leans toward me for a kiss, which was the softest kiss I ever had. With our eyes closed, our lips meet as we embrace in a kiss. We seemed to be in sync as our hearts beat like a drummer playing in a band. He slid his hands around my waist, up my back, down to my ass and cupped my cheeks. I felt his dick rising with excitement as my clit pulsated between my legs. He pulled away for a second to place the blanket on the sand. Grabbing me back closer and tighter he placed soft kisses around my neck. With his help I pulled off my cover-up while my body was filled with surge and anticipation. Laying me back, he removed my bikini top as my titties popped out waiting to feel his touch. He sucked my nipples with extreme intensity making sure to give both of them attention.

I was so wet as he got on top of me grinding and pressing his dick harder on my pussy. I wanted to feel him deep inside of me, as I pulled my bikini panties down toward my knees. He took off his pants, and I grabbed his dick stroking it gently in my hand. My juices were flowing like a stream in a river. With the tip of his dick he played with my middle. I spread my legs wider waiting for him to fill up the spot, but instead he placed his head between my legs. I was in total ecstasy as he sucked up my warm juices flowing from below. When he finally came up for air he knew I wanted more.

My pussy was screaming and crying out his name. He looked into my eyes, kissing me as he guided his dick deep inside. His dick was so big but he was gentle making sure not to rip my center. With the tip of his dick he pushed it in slowly until I could feel him pressed against walls inside. I let out a long sensual moan as our bodies moved to the same tune. In and out of my pussy he went pushing further deep inside until my lips gripped tighter around his dick. He closed his eyes enjoying the pleasure from within. Pushing my legs apart he started to move faster and pump harder. I started to yell in a fit of passion when he hit my g-spot. He felt it too as both of our bodies moved like a tidal wave in an ocean. I'm coming I yelled as he gripped my ass pulling my body closer. Oh shit he said as we both screamed together in pure pleasure. He collapsed on top of me as we both tried to catch our breath. My juices flowed all over the blanket as if the ocean washed up on the beach. He held me tight as we kissed under the moonlight.

Rrrrg Rrrrg was the last thing I could hear as I fumbled to hit the snooze button on the alarm clock. I laid in my bed, trying to hold onto my dream wishing my mystery man was here with me, in me. As I rolled over I felt a warm wet spot beneath my ass. Was it all a dream or did I piss in my bed? ...

AD-DICK

Lynx

"Hello, you have reached Yasmine Smith with Oppong Real Estate. Please leave your name, number and brief message; I will call you back." … *Beep*. "Yasmine where are you? You missed some appointments yesterday. I hope everything is okay. This is Cheryl call me back."

CHAPTER 1

I can't believe this traffic. Hopefully James will still be waiting for me to sign these papers. He's a really nice-looking older man thought Yasmine as she pressed down on the horn. "Damn people can't drive in Atlanta!" she yelled, looking in the rearview mirror in order to give the driver behind her a nasty gesture. Inspecting herself in the mirror she applied more Mac lip gloss to her already-glistening lips. I really don't need all of this because I already look gorgeous. Whew! Finally I made it to my destination in one piece she thought swinging her brand new pearl-white Maybach in the driveway. She stepped out of the car feeling like a celebrity. Hopefully his wife isn't with him today, because I need some time alone with her husband.

"You look gorgeous already," James said when he saw her brushing her hair in the mirror of the car's sun visor. Yasmine smiled pretending she didn't see him. "Well James, you're here early today?" She bent over struggling to remove the For Sale sign when James came behind her. "Let me help you with that." "Why thank you. Is your wife with you today?" "She couldn't make it today, she wasn't feeling good." "Well I hope she will get better. But, you can sign your half of the paperwork today and tell your wife to stop by my office tomorrow morning. You have purchased a beautiful home," she said opening the front door. *Now I just need to bless it* she thought.

Okay before I start sexing this man really good, which is the only way I know how. Let me first introduce myself. My name is Yasmine Smith, and I am the best realtor Atlanta, GA, has to offer. My client list includes politicians, rappers, lawyers, doctors, actors, and just everyday people with plenty of money to spend. I only work with the most prominent people in Atlanta because I am the best. That man about to sign his life away for this mansion is James. He doesn't have a clue of the treat I am about to give him. He may not want to go home to his wife after this experience, and one thing for sure -- he will be back for more.

I know you're thinking I'm a whore or a slut, but I'm neither. You see the difference from a whore and myself is: they get paid to fuck random men. They may get a little money once in a while but they do not earn nearly as much as I do. And most whores have a pimp they have to give their hard earned money to. I don't have a pimp. I just love to fuck men with money. And when I say money I don't mean the regular Joe blow that is on the corner selling dope, but my men have to have long, old money. New money is good but that old money lasts a lifetime. My pussy is worth a million dollars. And most of the men I sex I have to be attracted to. It really doesn't matter to me if they are married, have a girlfriend, or boyfriend. Once I set my eyes on my prize then I am determined to make them my next victim. Hell I've fucked most of my clients at least twice: once when they sign their loan papers and the second time when I let them enjoy the pleasure between my thighs. So technically they have been fucked over twice and I still get paid. I get very horny when my clients sign their loan papers. I immediately start adding up my commission and get excited.

And ladies this isn't about me not having a man, because I do. My fiancé is very handsome and successful, but he can't possibly satisfy my every need. Hell I'm a woman that enjoys a variety of choices and my clients offer me a variety. Well now that you know my story, I have to go back to my client James because my libido is jumping and we have to bless his new house! I made myself wet just thinking about fucking him.

"So does everything look okay?" she asked leaning over James to expose her lace Victoria's Secret bra. "Yeah everything looks good, especially you," said James placing his hand on her leg. Yasmine slid his hand up more so he could feel between her legs. "I really would like to have a piece of you," he said rubbing the inside of her thighs. *I was hoping you would!*

"First let me make sure the door is locked." Yasmine checked the bolt lock on the door, and then pulled the safety lock over it making sure no one could get in. She began swaying her hips motioning a strip tease. She slowly undressed, unbuttoning her blouse and slowly pulling down her skirt, tossing them both to the floor. She stood in front of him with her bra and panties on, loving the attention. James mouth dropped open; he was enjoying every minute of her striptease. She walked over and straddled him in the chair he was sitting in, softly kissing his neck while unbuttoning his shirt. Yasmine grinded her warm forest on him as she felt his dick getting harder. He feels like he is working with something down there. She stood up so she could unzip his pants. Helping him wiggle half way out of them she grabbed hold of his dick and the stroking party was on. "Are you ready for Yasmine?" she asked while removing her hands so she could take off the remaining garments. She removed off her bra and threw her panties in his face.

James quickly pulled down his pants. He didn't waste any time as he lifted her up and sat her on top of the desk putting her legs in the air. "Yes, fuck me," yelled Yasmine! "Oh daddy is going to fuck you real good," he said. *Daddy? I know this mutherfucker didn't just say daddy, and he just came. What the fuck! Shit that was a waste of my time.* "Damn baby you made me cum too fast." *No that wasn't me that was your lame ass* she thought as she went to the bathroom. "So when can I see you again?" he asked.

"Soon." As he learned over to give her a kiss, Yasmine turned her head away. "Sorry, James, I don't kiss," He looked hurt by her response but didn't say anything as they walked out of the house. "And don't forget to have your wife stop by the office to sign the rest of the paperwork." Yasmine jumped in her car and sped away. She looked at her watch. "Shit! I'm late for my dinner date with Isaac."

CHAPTER 2

"Hey baby sorry I am late for dinner. My client was not on time to sign the paperwork."

" I called your cell phone." "Really? My phone didn't ring. I probably wasn't getting any reception."

"I figured you would be hungry and ordered for you."

Now Isaac is my man and he is definitely 100 percent of a man. He has his own law firm and gives me whatever I want. So why do I like fucking other men? Well I've been fucking since I was twelve years old and I just enjoy the feeling. But I haven't met anyone that can bring me to the point where I'm ready to explode. Usually the man will cum and after that, it's over. I've never had an orgasm so you could say I'm looking for that one man that will make my pussy jump with excitement and leave me wanting more. Isaac is a great provider, but we rarely have sex. And when we do, he either can't get it up or he's too damn rough. Not sure what that is about because I am every man's dream woman. My skin is smooth and chocolate. I have long, black hair down my back. And it isn't a weave. I take pride in my body, which by the way is shaped like an hour-glass, and yes, I am very arrogant.

Isaac said he has some type of medical condition. At this point in the game it really doesn't matter because we will be married in less than six months and I will get half of all his assets. So the fact that he can't make me have an orgasm or fuck me when needed doesn't matter. I know plenty of men that will love to have sex with me when I want it. And there is one of them now. "Hello Charles, how are you doing?" "What's up Charles?" said Isaac. "How is the family?" "The family is doing great," Charles said.

"Are you in the market to buy a new condo anytime soon? We have some great deals," Yasmine offered.

"Excuse her, Charles. You know Yasmine is always trying to make money," Issac said.

"Yeah I know but I am looking to purchase a vacation home." Charles said. "See baby I know my clients. Well stop by the office when you are ready," Yasmine said. "I sure will. It's good seeing you both. Isaac we will have to get together soon for a game of golf." "That's what I'm talking about; just call me when you're ready," said Isaac. Yes, Charles was one of my many varieties of choices. Like cupcakes. He works for Congress and is well respected in Atlanta. It's our little secret and I know he would never tell.

"You look very sexy tonight baby," said Isaac as he rubbed Yasmine's leg. "Thank you baby. You know you have a sexy woman." Damn I know Isaac is horny but I really don't want to do anything tonight, especially since I just had sex. *The restaurant isn't that packed tonight* thought Yasmine looking around as she slowly slid underneath the table. Isaac laid back as he felt Yasmine unzipping his pants. There is my baby, she thought, grabbing his dick like it was her personalized joystick. Mmmmm, I love sucking my man's dick. I love the way his toes curl when he is about to explode in my mouth. Yasmine was sucking and licking when she heard the waiter come by the table. Isaac jumped which caused her to accidentally bite his dick. "Ouch!" he yelled.

"Are you okay sir?" asked the waiter. "Yeah, you scared me." "Would you like any dessert?"

"No, just the bill." Yasmine started kissing his dick. "Baby I am so sorry," she whispered. She felt him relaxing when she started sucking his dick real hard, squeezing her cheeks in like a vacuum, putting his entire dick in her mouth as if she was about to swallow him whole. She felt Isaac tense up as she went faster and faster, rubbing his shaft with one hand and massaging his balls in the other hand. "Oh shit!" she heard him say before exploding in her mouth. She swallowed every drop. *And that ladies is how you suck a dick. Hell I need to teach a class and call it, "How To Suck a Dick 101."* My man is satisfied, and I can go home to get some sleep. Yasmine slid back into her seat as quietly as she slid under the table. No one noticed she was gone, not even the waiter when he came back with the check. "I love you baby," said Isaac. Yasmine just smiled. I guess tomorrow I will have that necklace with the black diamonds that I've been asking for because my man has been spoiling me lately.

As they were leaving the restaurant, Yasmine starred in one spot as if she was in a trance. She was starring so hard like a deer caught in headlights that she almost walked into a chair. He was a tall, dark chocolate brother with muscles rippling through his t-shirt. I have to find out who he is she thought, not noticing Isaac was walking in the direction of the handsome stranger. Yasmine stood mesmerized, taking in everything about him from his shoes, wedding band, goatee, and his hair that was trimmed with precision.

"Hey, man, glad to see you made it safely," said Isaac. "This is my fiancé Yasmine, Atlanta's hottest realtor. This is my frat brother Dallas Jackson; remember I told you he was relocating here from Chicago a few months ago." Yasmine was speechless as she extended her hand out to shake his. He turned around and there was a woman standing behind him. Yasmine noticed she was more gorgeous than he was. "How did two gorgeous people end up together"she thought. "This is my wife Monica,"Dallas said. Monica fit right in with Atlanta's elite. She looked like she just stepped out of a magazine in her black Gucci dress that looked like it was painted on her body, nude Christian Louboutin shoes and Gucci handbag. Yes I did notice her. Hell who wouldn't have? She looked like a model: light skinned, baby-blue eyes … high-yellow heifer thought Yasmine. With only a smile still plastered on her face, Yasmine had not uttered a word since being introduced to them. "Are you still looking for a house?" asked Isaac."Yeah but we haven't had any luck," Dallas answered. "My babe can help you find something nice. Babe, give Dallas a card." Yasmine felt like she woke up out of a trance when she felt Isaac nudging her. "Why, of course, it would be my pleasure to help you find a place to live. Atlanta is a beautiful place and I can find whatever you are looking for from art deco to a mansion of your desire." "Okay, thanks. I will give you a call next week," said Dallas. "It was a pleasure meeting you both," said Monica.

At home Yasmine still couldn't get Dallas off her mind as she undressed to take a shower. Isaac was talking but she didn't hear anything he was saying. I have never wanted someone as bad as I want Dallas. Isaac came up behind her interrupting her thoughts kissing on her neck. "Are you okay babe?" Issac asked. She gave him a passionate kiss thrusting her tongue in his mouth imagining he was Dallas. She began to grind her pussy against his leg. "Baby I love you so much," he said as he started sucking on her riped supple breast. Yasmine was still trying to think about Dallas but Isaac was making it very hard. She loved Isaac but he didn't do it for her when it came to sex. Sex with him was like being in a jail fight, where the guy is trying hard to protect his asshole from the other guy trying to fuck him. Damn this isn't working for me but I've got him aroused. Hell, he may cum on himself. She started moving just as fast as he did. He threw her on the bed putting one leg in the air and holding the other leg under his weight. He was going so hard and fast she couldn't keep up. My pussy isn't even wet and after this it's going to feel like a rug burn.Here I go faking my moaning and groaning. "Oooh, yes baby!" Don't judge me I have to do this so he will think I'm satisfied. Uh oh here we go! ... One, two, three, four ... hold up four pumps. He would've had an orgasm by the third pump. Five "oh shit baby, I'm cummin'!" he yelled. And it's over. Isaac passed out on top of her breathing heavily. "You are the best baby."Rolling her eyes she got up and went back in the bathroom to take her shower. *I think I have an appointment tomorrow with that fine ass Falcon linebacker Damien Martin. Whew, can't wait.*

CHAPTER 3

"Good morning,Yasmine." "Morning Cheryl. Do I have any messages?" "No, but you do have a guest in your office." "Who is it?" "Tyrone." "Okay, thanks."

Great. What the hell does Mr. Banks want? He was so clingy during our affair. And not to mention he stalked me for a couple of months. I know it was wrong to mess with him considering we worked together, but I couldn't resist. He was so sexy and seemed to have everything together. But he had the nerve to blame me for his wife leaving him. I didn't put a gun to his head and make him have sex with me.

Seeing him sitting at my desk made my skin crawl. Slamming the door behind her, "so what do you want Tyrone?" "Damn, I thought you would be happy to see me." "Now why would you think that?" she asked sarcastically. "Well to be honest I missed you and wanted to see if we can have dinner soon."

"Tyrone I'm sorry but we are over. I thought I made that clear six months ago." He reached across her desk and grabbed her wrist twisting it. "Look, Yasmine, you owe me more than this shit! We had something and I lost everything because of my affair with you." "Tyrone, I don't owe you shit! You knew it was only sex from the beginning. It wasn't my fault you were stupid and let your wife find out about us." Tyrone was about to raise his hand to hit her when her assistant Cheryl walked in. "Is everything okay?" "Yeah, Cheryl, Mr. Banks was just leaving." "Good seeing you Cheryl, and Yasmine this conversation isn't over." "What is his problem?" asked Cheryl. "Nothing. You know Mr. Banks has some issues."

Yasmine started thinking back to how everything fell apart with Tyrone. He did eat my pussy better than any man I've been with. Hell

71

I may have had one orgasm with him. Once his wife found out he was having an affair, he insisted that I leave Isaac for him. The only reason his wife found out about us is because he never deleted his text messages. She saw everything in his blackberry, even the dates when we met. She almost caught us in the act one day while at his house. She came home early and I just managed to leave out of the back door before all hell broke loose. Still not sure how he got fired but he said his wife called and told the boss about our affair. I had to think fast and told the boss he was sexually harassing me. I didn't think they would fire him, but he can't blame me for him losing his job. I had to look out for myself and make sure Isaac never found out what happened.

At first Tyrone was okay with losing his job. He was a good agent and would be able to find another job. I learned a lot from him, but when he realized we couldn't see each other anymore he started acting crazy. I thought he had moved on until he came by the office today. Oh damn, it's lunch time already, and I can't miss my meeting with Mr. Damien Martin. *Ladies, he is fine with a nice tight ass.* "I'll be back, I have a meeting," she told Cheryl. Yasmine got in her car not noticing Tyrone was sitting in his car watching her. As she pulled off he followed her. *I wonder if Damien really needs my services or does he just want to have sex. Whatever he wants it doesn't matter because that brother is gorgeous. I'll kiss the ground he walks on any day.*

Yasmine got out of the car with her briefcase in hand. "Hey beautiful," said Damien as he met her in the driveway to give her a hug. Yasmine never noticed Tyrone following her. Sitting in his car he immediately started taking pictures from his cell phone. "You look good as always Yasmine." "Thanks. So is this business or pleasure?" Damien just smiled showing his deep dimples in his right cheek. "A little of both, do you want something to drink?" "Yeah, a glass of Moscato would be nice." She was about to say something when she was interrupted by another male voice. "Yasmine, this is Mark." "Hello." *And ladies he was fine as well. Damn I didn't know Atlanta had this many fine ass men in one city but it is called Hot'lanta. This many mean double trouble for me.*

"So Damien what are you looking for?" "Not sure yet but if the price is right then I will purchase it," he winked. "Do you want to stay in the city or on the outskirts of Atlanta?" "It doesn't matter," he said while getting on his knees. "We can talk about this later," as he took the pen and notepad from her hand. He started to kiss her when she turned her head. "Oh I forgot you don't like to kiss. Well I'll kiss your other lips."

Yasmine was sitting in the chair with her legs spread apart as her clit started jumping with excitement. Damien pulled her panties down as she slid her skirt up. "Mmmmm," she moaned when Damien placed his soft lips on her labia, darting his tongue in and out her vagina. His tongue went over her shaft and clit, as he sucked up her juices. He was going back and forth with his tongue over her clit and in her vagina as if he wasn't sure which one made him happier. She was enjoying every second as she took off her blazer and felt someone's hand on her shoulder. She looked up and saw it was Mark. He didn't ask to join but that didn't matter to Yasmine. Having two men fuck her wasn't something she did all the time but when she was in the mood she enjoyed it.

Mark was already naked as he helped Yasmine take off her blouse. He started sucking her nipples while Damien was still eating her pussy. Her pussy was wet like a faucet, and she couldn't wait to feel both of them inside of her. With her head leaned back she grabbed Mark's dick and started sucking it and grabbing his balls. Up and down she sucked when Damien got up and took off his clothes. She had Mark's dick rock hard as he directed her towards the couch. She laid back as Mark slid his thick shaft in her wet pussy. It felt like he hit the bottom of her pussy as her lips gripped his dick tight. He was stroking it, making sure to press against her clit each time. She let out a long moan but made sure Damien wasn't neglected. Mark was fucking her good but her appointment was with Damien. Damien stood over top of her while she sucked his dick. She was trying to concentrate on Damien when she felt Mark cumming all over her.

"Turnover," said Damien. She leaned over the couch with her ass in the air as Damien fought to put his dick in her ass. The sensation she felt from Damien was more intense than when Mark was in her pussy. She arched her back with her knees pressed on the sofa. Mark still wanted more; some kind of way he maneuvered underneath of her. Yasmine allowed her legs to part in a splitting position so both men were in a hole. Their bodies were going in unison and Damien was the lead. Yasmine loved every minute of it. Her body was consumed with so much intensity as Mark sucked on each of her nipples. Not sure if they could feel each other inside of her but they definitely felt each other on the outside as they fucked her in each hole their nut sacks grazed against one another causing them to cum at the same time. Both of their bodies jerked with passion. Damien started pulling her ass further towards him as Mark tried to keep his dick inside of her pussy. Yasmine didn't know if they were going to split her holes into one. Damien pulled his dick out spewing cum all over her back as she continued fucking Mark until he came again. "Damn," said Damien. "Baby you need to package you pussy up and sell it," said Mark. Tyrone was standing in the window shocked and furious he couldn't join the trio. He took so many pictures his camera phone couldn't take anymore.

Yasmine went to take a shower. She started putting on her clothes and overheard Damien and Mark talking about what just happened. They were ecstatic and she felt pleased with the outcome. Damn, after all that fucking I still didn't have an orgasm. I may need to make an appointment with my doctor or psychiatrist. She interrupted their conversation, "so Mark will you be looking for a house anytime soon?" asked Yasmine. He was still laying on the couch naked with a towel thrown over him. "Yeah I could use your service all the time. "I've been told," she said winking her eye at Damien as he walked he walked her outside. I'll be calling you soon," yelled Mark said taking her business card. "Talk to you soon," said Damien." *Whew, I need to go home and take a nap that was too much at lunch time.* She transferred all of her calls and went home.

Still not noticing Tyrone following her she pulled up to her parking garage to park her car. Yasmine sat in the car for a second with the garage door open, texting one of her clients. As she stepped out of the car someone grabbed her arm putting his hand over her mouth. She could tell by the smell of his cologne it was Tyrone. "Yeah, bitch, I have pictures of you getting your freak on with an Atlanta Falcons linebacker!" Tyrone pulled out the camera and showed her the pictures he had taken. "I lost my family and job behind a whore! You fucking bitch! If you don't want these pictures to get back to your faithful fiancé then you will do whatever I ask. And it's going to start by me fucking you."

Yasmine didn't yell or scream as Tyrone ripped off her skirt and panties raping her in the garage. "Tomorrow I want you to give me five hundred thousand dollars and I want that pussy again!" Grabbing her face, he kissed her in the mouth. Yasmine fell on her knees and cried spitting the taste of him from out of her mouth. *I can't believe that bastard is blackmailing me!* She ran in the house, and immediately jumped in the shower trying to erase Tyrone's scent from her body. I wish that affair with Tyrone never happened! I have to get those pictures back at whatever cost.

Sitting on the side of the bed she tried to figure out a way to get the pictures from Tyron without paying him. This is too much to deal with right now. Isaac will be home soon and he will know something is bothering me if I don't get myself together. I just heard his car pull up but why is there another car pulling up behind him. I don't feel like socializing with anyone tonight. Yasmine laid back down pretending to be asleep when she heard Isaac talking loudly to another male she didn't recognize.

"Babe, I'm home," Issac yelled to Yasmine. "Make yourself at home I'll be right back," he said to his guests. Yasmine was still pretending to be asleep when she felt Isaac leaning over to kiss her. "Hey beautiful, wake up we have company." "Isaac I don't feel like entertaining anyone tonight, and why didn't you call to let me know you were bringing company home?" "I'm sorry it was last minute. It's just Dallas and his wife Monica." Yasmine felt a spark of energy when she heard Dallas's name. You don't have to do anything. I will put some steaks on the grill while you be the wonderful hostess you are. "Okay, give me a moment to get myself together because my head is really hurting."

When Isaac left out of the room, Yasmine rummaged through her closet like a mad woman. I have to find something sexy yet comfortable so Dallas will notice me. She finally decided to put on a pair of jean shorts with a tank top that shows her belly ring. Grabbing the bottle of Moscato from the wine cooler with four glasses, she headed toward the patio. "Hello, and welcome to our home," she said.

"Hey, Yasmine," said Dallas. Yasmine handed everyone a glass and poured the wine. She looked around and noticed Monica was sitting quiet in a corner. "Hey girl is everything okay?" Yasmine asked.

"Yeah, just tired. It's been a really long day. I had four photo shoots," Monica answered. "Okay, so you are a model?" "Yes." "I knew it when I first saw you. I thought to myself, 'she is gorgeous and has to be a model.'" "Thank you," said Monica smiling. "Your house is beautiful and this patio is so relaxing. This is something we would like to have in our home." "Have you had any luck in finding a place yet?" Yasmine asked Monica. "No, because I've had a lot of photo shoots lately and haven't had the time. I left it up to Dallas but you know men take their time with everything." "Yes, I know the feeling. Well I'm available whenever you are ready." "Did you hear that Dallas? Yasmine is willing to help us find a home ASAP! Okay I think I still have your card. Can we meet up tomorrow around one o'clock?"

"Yes that will work for me; If anything change I will let you know."

Yasmine could not take her eyes off Dallas. Watching him made her forget about being raped by Tyrone. "He is very handsome isn't he," Monica asked? "Excuse me, who are you talking about?" Yasmine inquired shocked by Monica's question. "Dallas. It's no problem, women stare at him all the time," said Monica as she put her hand on Yasmine's leg. "Sorry Monica, but I was looking at my man Isaac." "Oh, I'm sorry. I'm so used to women looking at Dallas." "Well, he is very handsome, but I only have eyes for Isaac." Yasmine noticed Monica's hand was still on her leg, which she politely moved.

"Oh I'm sorry, so when is the wedding?" "In six months, and I can't wait to be his wife." "That is wonderful and I'm sure the wedding will be the talk of Atlanta." Yasmine didn't think about that, but Isaac was well known and she was the best real estate agent on this side of Cobb County. Yes, there will be a lot of prominent guests at the wedding. That will give me a reason to find the perfect dress, and I can't wait. Okay now I'm not sure what is up with Monica but she seems a little too feely, touchy for me. She keeps touching my damn leg. I'm used to this shit from a man not a woman. Maybe it is the wine but if she puts her hand on my thigh one more damn time I'm going to knock her ass out! I don't want her, but I do want her man.

Isaac finished the steaks and made a salad to go with the meal. There wasn't a lot of conversation over dinner. Yasmine was thinking of a way to get the pictures back from Tyrone without paying him any money. Isaac was shoving his food down like it was his last meal. She glanced over at Monica and Dallas who were both starring out into space. They must be going through something because I sense a lot of tension between those two. After dinner they sat around listening to the new CD by Chrisette Michelle.

"I need to meet this girl because I love all of her songs," said Yasmine. "Yeah, she has a hot CD," Dallas chimed in. "So how was Isaac in college?" Yasmine asked making idle conversation with Dallas. "Huh?" Dallas asked looking puzzled. "Isaac, was he a player in college? Oh naw, he was a real quite brother until we broke him down during pledging." " Pledging? Oh really, what fraternity?"

"The Alpha's of course," Isaac said all proud and shit. Twisting my lips in disbelief I can't imagine Dallas pledging a fraternity. *Hell he never mentioned being in a fraternity and he only mentioned Dallas a few weeks ago* she thought. She was about to ask him some more questions about Isaac when Dallas abruptly said they had to go. "Sorry we have to eat and run, but we have to go walk the dog. We had a great time tonight," said Dallas. "Yasmine, I will call you tomorrow." *Yes please do she thought.*

"Maybe the two of us can go shopping soon," said Monica as she rubbed Yasmine's arm. There she goes again, touching me. Yasmine just smiled gritting her teeth. Thanks, but no thanks, she thought. I'm soooo glad she's leaving. She shivered while turning her body slightly, gesturing that she didn't want to be touched as she waved good night.

CHAPTER 4

Yasmine jumped out of bed when she realized she was late for the office. She looked around and saw Isaac had already left for work. When she went to get in her car she noticed a note on the windshield that said, "Don't forget my money you whore or your whole world will fall apart!" How did this bastard get in my house?! Isaac must have left the garage door open after he left. This is getting out of hand, but I can't think about this right now. I have to get myself together for my appointment.

Her phone was ringing but the caller ID showed the number was unavailable. She picked up the phone. "Hello. Hey bitch did you get my note?" Tyrone said on the other end. She didn't say anything. "Well meet me with my money by Friday or else your fiancé will find out what kind of skank you really are. Enjoy your day." Yasmine hung up the phone. She was about to throw it out the window when it rang again. "Do not call me again!" she yelled. "Excuse me, Yasmine, this is Dallas." "I am so sorry. Someone was playing on my phone." "Are you okay?" "Yes I'm fine. Thanks for asking. How can I help you?"

"I wanted to see if we could change our appointment to two o'clock today." "Okay, that will work. I have a couple of properties to show you, and I would like to make sure I have the keys ready." "Alright, I will see you then."

Yasmine forgot about being blackmailed by Tyrone as she daydreamed about Dallas on her way to work. Damn my pussy is getting wet just from daydreaming about him. "Good morning, Cheryl. Do I have any messages?" "No but a package was outside the office this morning with just your name on it. I put it on your desk." "Okay thanks."

She walked in her office and saw an 8 x 10-inch manila envelope on her desk with no return address. Not knowing what she would find in the package, she started feeling palpitations, anticipating what could be the contents. Opening the envelope, she gasped in shock as pictures fell out. There were pictures of her with every man she had sex with including Tyrone. This has to be Tyrone but why would he include a picture of himself and how would he know about the other men? Some of these pictures were taken before I met Tyrone. This bastard must have known about me before we became involved. There was even a picture of her assistant Cheryl's ex fiancé. Yasmine quickly put the pictures back in the envelope and put them in her briefcase. Cheryl knocked on the door, came in and gave Yasmine her usual cup of coffee. "Here you go, it's your favorite cup of coffee. Are you okay? You look flushed," Cheryl said. "I'm just tired we had to entertain some guests last night." "Okay, well don't forget your eleven a.m. appointment with Mr. and Mrs. Gregory. They are such a cute old couple. Yeah, I think they are going to love their new senior community."

Yasmine looked at Cheryl with a deep suspicion. Tyrone has to have someone else helping him because he is not smart enough to do this by himself. Yasmine decided to get some fresh air and leave the office until it was time for her appointment with the Gregory's; she took the coffee and headed out the back door. She sat in her car and examined each picture. These were all taken at the houses I sold. But how and who would know what I was doing and when? *Bzzzz* her phone vibrated in the cup holder. Cheryl sent her a text message saying that Mr. Gregory wanted to reschedule his appointment for today and will call back when he can. Using that information she decided to do some investigating and search some of the houses she had on the market. I need to see if a camera is in any of those houses.

Searching high and low she didn't find a camera on the premises. I wonder if maybe Cheryl is helping Tyrone. They used to joke all the time at work. She is the only one that knew what houses I was showing and on what particular days. I take my calendar home but I know Isaac isn't interested in my work. Hell, we never even talk about our jobs once we get home. Looking down at her watch, shit I only have fifteen minutes left to meet Dallas. For some reason, he wanted to have lunch first to discuss his options. I definitely have some options for him: missionary, doggie style, sixty-nine, milkshake whatever his pleasure. Pulling up to the restaurant Dallas was sitting outside on the patio looking delectable. "Sorry I'm late. Are you doing okay?" she asked. "I'm good and you look terrific." Hmmm he gave me a compliment so he must be interested. "Thanks." I wasn't hungry but decided to order a salad while I listened to him. "Look I've seen a few houses around town that interest me but I'm not sure what we want." "That is not a problem. I will promise to find what you are looking for." Yasmine looked in her briefcase and noticed Dallas was staring at her. "Is everything okay?" "Yeah I'm just wondering how in the world Isaac found a woman as fine as you." "Thank you. Isaac is a good man but it was a lot of work for him to make me his woman," she laughed. He isn't wasting anytime flirting with me. "So, do you want to live in the city or the outskirts of Atlanta?" She gazed into his eyes waiting for a reply.

"You know, Yasmine, I never thought about it, but I would love for you to show me your recommendations." "Great, I have a few houses to show you. Would you like to ride with me or follow me?" "I'll ride with you. I want to see how it feels to ride in a Maybach." "It's just like any other ride just smoother."

They were having a good conversation in the car when Yasmine received another anonymous phone call. "Hello, hello, hello." but no one said anything. Looking around she thought Tyrone was following her. *Oh hell this is useless; I didn't even notice him following me the other day.* Well I hope he will take notes when he sees me fucking Dallas. "We are finally here. I apologize; the traffic is not usually this bad during this time of day." "Yeah I thought traffic would be better in Atlanta." "No it's always congested," she said while fumbling with the lock on the door. "Here let me help you with that," said Dallas. She was so close to him her lips brushed past his neck. *Take me now* she thought. "There you go," he said as the door opened to the foyer.

"This is nice and I like the colors." "Yeah and this house will not be on the market for long. Do you think Monica would like it?" "Probably, but it's so big for just the two of us." "Well I'm sure you all will be having some babies soon." "Not sure about that. Monica is into her career and will not have any babies messing up that body. She will probably like it if the bedroom is what she wants. It has to be big enough for her and have a closet large enough for all of her clothes." "Well let's go upstairs and see the bedroom." "Wow! The master bedroom is like an apartment. Do you see how big it is?" he said grabbing her hand to escort her in the master bedroom. "I'm sure they have houses just like this in Chicago."

"Yeah but they are more expensive." Dallas didn't waste any time as he grabbed her by the waist and held her close. "Yasmine I have wanted you since the first time we met." "What about Isaac," asked Yasmine?

"I won't tell if you won't tell." he said grabbing her ass in the palm of his hands and lifted her up laying her body gently on the bed. Yasmine tried to help as he took off her skirt but he was in control.

Just lay back and enjoy, he said. Her pussy was jumping anticipating feeling Dallas inside of her. He took off all her clothes and stood over top of her looking like he was taking a mental picture in his brain. He unbuttoned his shirt with one hand as he led his other hand between her legs putting his fingers deep inside of her pussy. Her juices were already beginning to flow as he took off his wife beater and jeans. He had the body of a track star, lean but very muscular. He stood there rubbing his dick while his other hand was still deep inside of her. She was ready for him, but he got on top of her kissing softly around her neck and making his way to her breast. Giving each breast special attention he sucked her nipples and still stimulating her clit with his hand. He didn't miss a spot on her body as he kissed his way down to her pussy. He ate her pussy sucking on her clit for what seemed like an hour. Her body was jumping with excitement. He finished by kissing her inner thighs and sucking her toes. He turned her over and started kissing her butt softly making his way towards her anus. Yasmine started feeling something she had never felt before and her body jerked and she yelled out his name, "Oh Dallas!" It was then he knew her body was ready to feel all of him inside of her. She got on her knees as he spread her legs apart. She felt his dick finding its way deep inside her pussy taking him all inside of her. He knew how to stroke his dick deep inside as he smacked her on the ass. It felt so good to feel Dallas inside of her, she squeeze her vagina lips tight around his dick making sure to back her ass up. "Oh shit baby!" He started fucking her harder and harder. Yasmine couldn't hold back as her body tensed up and she yelled the word she wanted to yell for years, "I'm cumming!"

Even though she came her body still wanted more. Dallas was the first man that made her have an orgasm and she wanted to feel it again and again. She layed back as he got on top spreading her legs apart like a seesaw. "Yes, Dallas" she yelled as she felt her clit popping. They both climaxed together. Yasmine lay there with Dallas still on top of her feeling like she was in heaven. "So that is what an orgasm feels like," she thought as she felt her pussy still doing somersaults. I want more of him but Dallas was getting up as she tried playing with his dick. "Whew, you are the best," he said. "No you are because that is the first time I've ever had an orgasm."

"Are you serious?" he asked looking shocked. He bent down to kiss her and she didn't resist. "Come on let's get dressed so I can see the other houses." "Yeah we've already missed an hour." She looked around before leaving the house to make sure no one was outside. "You okay?" he asked. "Yeah just thinking about what just happened." "Well I hope this won't be the last time." "Definitely not! Mr. Jackson. Come on let's go."

Yasmine enjoyed her time with Dallas but she was feeling nervous because she didn't know if Tyrone was somewhere lurking around. "I had a good time today and liked all of the houses I saw. Maybe next time I'll bring Monica along and then we'll make our final decision." "I enjoyed you as well." Yasmine could not stop smiling as she drove home. Nothing can spoil my evening. She pulled in the driveway and Isaac was already home. Damn why is he home so early. Opening the front door she was surprised to see rose petals on the floor; she followed them all the way upstairs where they stopped at the bathroom. Candles surrounded the tub that was filled with her favorite aroma, lavender bath oil. "Awww baby you treat me so good." "Hey beautiful I thought you could use a relaxing evening. I hope Dallas didn't keep you on your feet all day." An image of Dallas fucking her with her feet in the air flashed through her mind, "Nope but I think he may be interested in one of the houses he saw. We will probably go out again tomorrow." *At least I hope so she thought.* Isaac took off her clothes and led her to the tub. This feels so good. He undressed and joined her in the tub. Damn he would want to have sex on the same day I had my first orgasm. "I can't wait to make you my wife," he said kissing her neck.

"Yeah me too" "Turn around and let me see that beautiful face." Yasmine turned around facing him as the water dripped down her body. Let me just say this ladies, I really do love Isaac but he just doesn't do it for me sexually. I think I may be in love with Dallas. Isaac started kissing on her breast as he caressed her body. "Baby I'm sorry but I don't want to do anything tonight." With a disappointed look on his face he put the towel around his waist. "Okay well you relax and I will fix you something to eat." Yasmine was relieved when he left the bathroom. I don't need him spoiling me having my first orgasm. She wanted to call Dallas but when she picked up her phone she noticed he texted her, "enjoyed experiencing you today maybe we can meet up tomorrow." "Yes because my body wants to experience you again," she typed. Yasmine's text was interrupted by an anonymous call. She figured it had to be Tyrone. "Will you please stop calling me!" "Look, bitch, until I get my money I will call you every day.

So who was that guy you were with today? Don't get quiet now I saw everything. You are a nasty woman! Damn I'm starting to feel sorry for your man. Well you finish taking your bath because that pussy needs to be cleaned." How would that bastard know I'm taking a bath? Shocked and scared by his remark Yasmine jumped out of the tub. Without putting on her robe she ran downstairs naked. Isaac was in the kitchen cooking. "Are you okay baby?" "Yeah, I thought I heard you call my name." She went back upstairs checking every room. Not sure what she was looking for but she figured a camera had to be somewhere in the house. She looked in every room and didn't see anything. This is getting crazy. I need to tell Isaac what is going on and pray for his forgiveness. I'll ask Dallas his opinion tomorrow; maybe he can give me some advice.

CHAPTER 5

Isaac was still asleep when Yasmine left for work. She went by the bank to withdraw the funds so Tyrone would stop harassing her. She put the money in the trunk of her car and went to meet Dallas. Hmmm I know Tyrone will be mad he won't be able to take a picture of me in action. I'm glad Dallas decided to meet at a hotel. I feel a lot safer. She knocked on the door and Dallas opened the door looking better than he did yesterday. She dropped everything and started kissing him. "I see you are happy to see me," he said. "Yes I am," she said while unbuttoning her blouse. My body has been yearning for you since yesterday. Dallas didn't waste any time giving Yasmine what she wanted. He pulled her bra up grabbing her titties and sucked her nipples. "Dallas!" she moaned as she took off her clothes. They started kissing as they fell onto the bed. With the tip of his penis he rubbed her pussy and got instantly excited when he felt her juices. She got on top of him kissing his neck, chest, and sucking his dick as she rubbed his balls. Yasmine couldn't take it anymore as her pussy pulsated from excitement. She sat on his dick riding it like a cowgirl. "Dallas I'm cumming!" she yelled as her juices ran down his leg. Yasmine came but she didn't want Dallas to take his dick out of her. She clasped her pussy lips down never wanting to let go when she heard a woman's voice.

"I like the way you ride his dick." She turned around and was shocked to see his wife Monica sitting in the chair naked watching her fuck her husband. She sat with her legs wide open playing with her pussy.

"What the hell is going on?" "Calm down baby," Dallas said. "Yeah from the moment I saw you I told Dallas I couldn't wait to taste you," said Monica. Yasmine was curious and her body was still shaking from wanting to have another orgasm. "Do you mind if I join in?" She didn't say anything when Monica came over and started kissing on her body. She fell into submission as she lay there while both Monica and Dallas took turns eating her pussy. Monica was definitely better in this department because she knew exactly where to go to make her body scream for more. Dallas sat on top of her as she sucked his dick.

"I think I will call you juicy fruit." said Monica, "because your pussy is so juicy and sweet." Monica spread her lips apart wider as she went deeper inside with her tongue. Her body girated and she didn't care what they did to her. Dallas knew exactly what she wanted as he turned her over on her hands and knees. His dick was stroking her pussy so good she wanted to yell. "Have you ever tasted the cat?" asked Monica as she lay down in front of her exposing her wet brown pussy. Not knowing what to do she just starred at her couchie as Monica clasped her legs around her head forcing her down. Yasmine started kissing her pussy then sticking her tongue in her vagina. "Oooh," said Monica. Yasmine was licking Monica as Dallas continued fucking her. She could feel his dick tightening up as he was about to cum. They climaxed together but Dallas made sure to have enough for Monica as he got on top of her to finish the job. Yasmine looked in amazement and wondered to herself who was this couple. With Monica's legs stretched back like she was doing yoga Dallas put his dick in her asshole. "Yes. Baby!" she yelled in excitement as he squirted his cum all over her ass and pussy.

Yasmine went to the bathroom to take a shower and was shocked Dallas and Monica were still in bed together. "Don't leave we wanted to spend the entire day fucking you," said Monica. Okay this is too weird for me and I have to go. "Dallas, call me if you are still interested in the property we looked at the other day." "Okay," he mumbled as Monica started sucking his dick. She closed the door in a daze walking to her car. *What the hell just happened* she thought.

Walking to the car she felt someone walking close behind her. She was about to turn around when they grabbed her putting a hand over her mouth. "Open the trunk," said a man's voice. She tried to fight him off, but he was too big. "Is that the money?" She nodded. *This must be Tyrone but it doesn't feel like him.* He grabbed the suitcase out of the trunk and put a rag over her nose. She felt herself feeling woozy as he threw her in the trunk of the car. "Bye sweetheart. I've had a good time." The voice sounded familiar and she thought she saw Isaac's face before blacking out.

CHAPTER 6

When Yasmine finally woke up she was still in the trunk of her car. She yelled and screamed but no one came to her rescue. She finally remembered she always kept a spare key on her. She fumbled around in the dark feeling through her purse. After what felt like an hour she finally found the key. She pressed the unlocked button and the trunk popped open. She wasn't sure how long she was in the trunk until she looked at her watch; it was 7:00am the next day. She didn't know what to do or how to explain any of this shit to Isaac. She checked her phone and had several missed calls from her job but none from Isaac. She decided to go back to the room and try to get some help from Dallas and Monica. She knocked on the door and the cleaning lady was there. Damn they must have checked out. For some reason she decided to call Dallas's phone but the number was no longer in service. Needing to get their opinion on what to tell Isaac she drove to the hotel were Dallas and Monica were staying at.

"Hello I'm here to meet my brother and his wife Dallas and Monica Jackson. Can you call their room?" "Ma'am we don't have any guest by that name." That must be a mistake. She remembered Dallas say this was the hotel they were staying in until they could find a house. She jumped in her car and sped home. *Isaac must be worried sick* she thought. She called his phone but it went to the voicemail. "Hey baby. I am so sorry someone robbed me and threw me in the trunk of my car. I will explain everything when I get home and Isaac I do love you." *I know Isaac will understand everything.* She pulled up and didn't see his car in the garage and noticed a For Sale sign in the yard. *Who the hell put a For Sale sign in my yard? I'll deal with that later right now I need to relax and get a glass of wine.* She went in the house and everything was gone. She ran upstairs and the closets were cleaned out, including all of her clothes. The only thing left was a chair and table in the kitchen with an envelope. *Damn he must have found out about me and Dallas.*

She opened the envelope and it contained the pictures Tyrone was blackmailing her with. She noticed there were some added pictures that included her ménage trios with Dallas and Monica. How in the hell did Tyrone take these pictures? She also noticed another picture of Tyrone and Isaac kissing. What the fuck! This can't be happening! She called Isaac's job. "Hello may I please speak with Isaac King?"

"I'm sorry, no one by that name works here." "But he's an attorney." "Ma'am you have the wrong number." Curious about the For Sale sign in the yard, she called the number for the real estate agent. "Yes, can you tell me how long this house has been on the market?" "For the past six months. The previous owners got behind and couldn't afford it. Are you interested in looking at the home?" Hello…hello?" Yasmine held the phone in her hand speechless. She looked further in the envelope and there was a letter from Isaac:

"Dear Yasmine,

You are truly a work of art. I don't know how you can fuck all those men without a conscious. The straw that broke the camel's back is when my lover Tyrone fell for you. I couldn't let that happen. I know this all comes as a surprise to you, but I am his wife. We've been together since we were in jail together for robbing and conning beautiful women like yourself. We don't have any kids he just told that lie to make himself feel like a man. I came home that day and almost caught the two of you together but you like a coward ran out the back door. I've been plotting to get you back since that day. Next man you get involved with you might want to check and make sure he really has a job. You see I've never worked the entire time we were together and I spent all of your money. I could have carried the lie up until the wedding date, but it was too much. I couldn't bear having sex with you another day. Girl you are too much and I really missed my man Tyrone. You see we complete each other. And I guess you've figured out by now that there isn't a Dallas or Monica. They were just two people I met willing to make some money. They did a wonderful job and played you well. I applaud both of them. Dallas was so good you actually thought you were in love with him. LOL! You wouldn't know what love is if it slapped you in the face. Oh and I left the engagement ring because I know you like diamonds but babe that ring is made out of glass. Well take care of yourself and keep your damn legs closed! I'm sure you will find a way to get back on your feet or at least find a way to put them up in the air!"

She balled the letter up and threw it in the trash. Damn that bastard set me up and took all of my money! Well I hope he knows payback is a bitch and her name is Yasmine!

SUGA B.

Lynx

Suga raced out of her job, not paying attention to where she was going. Her eyes where focused down as she searched for her purse looking for her car keys. She didn't notice the gentleman in front of her as she bumped into him knocking all of his papers out of his hand. "I am so sorry," she said bending over to pick up the mess she made. "No problem.," he said. As she handed over his paper she noticed his large biceps and calves. She looked right at him and his smile lit up her heart. Damn he is handsome. I think these belong to you she said handing over the remainder of his paperwork. Thanks for your help, I didn't see you, said the handsome stranger. Suga didn't say anything as he spoke. She was taken in by his chiseled face and caramel complexion. It looked like his body was taken out of a fire and pounded by a nail and hammer to chisel him into the perfect man. He gave her a smile that showed the deepest dimples in his cheeks.

"Are you okay?" he asked. "I'm sorry, yes I'm fine." "Yes you are," he said flirting. Only thing she could do was smile. "Do you work out?" he asked. Before she could answer "yes" or "no," he said, "Take my card, I've started a fitness class in this building every Monday, Wednesday, and Friday after work. The first class is free but since I bumped into you I will give you the first three classes for free." "Okay, I will try to make one of your classes ... Troy?" she said glancing down at his card that had his name in bold letters. "Hope to see you at one of those free sessions." As she turned to walk away he said, "Excuse me but I didn't get your name?" "I'm sorry my name is Suga B." He had a puzzled look on his face. "My grandmother named me Suga because she said I was the sweetest little baby she had ever seen. And my last name is way too hard to pronounce so I use the first initial." She thought about what she said and prayed he would believe her. If she told him the real reason her name was Suga B. he would run for the hills … or offer her money for sex. Frank gave her the name Suga because when she was running tricks every man that tasted her pussy said it was sweet as sugar. "Well it was a pleasure to meet you, Miss Suga B," he said grabbing her hand to shake it. There was a jolt of electricity she felt when he touched her hand. "Have a good evening." "Thanks you do the same."

Driving home Suga's mind was on Troy. I would love for Troy the Trainer to train every inch of my body. That man is gorgeous and his face should be beside the word in the Dictionary! Her fantasies quickly diminished when she pulled up in her driveway. Here we go with the drama. Standing in front of the door she looked down at the mat that read, "Home, Sweet Home". That's a joke because there is nothing sweet about this home. She walked through the door. "Frank, I'm home!," she yelled. Instead of being greeted warmly he stormed out of nowhere yelling, "What the hell took you so long? You know I had some runs to make and needed to use the car." "I'm sorry I was stuck in traffic." "Yeah, it's always traffic! I should beat yo ass for making me late!" Suga started backing toward the door ready to make a dash as he got closer in her face. "And have my damn plate ready when I come home!" "Okay."

"What did you say?" he raged. "I mean, yes sir." He slammed the door so hard the painting fell off the wall. Suga was nervous as her body tensed up. This shit is ridiculous. Frank treats me like shit and I'm tired of taking his abuse. But what can I do, with no money saved and I don't have any relatives.

Looking in the mirror she didn't like the image that was looking back. Her long brown hair was always pulled back in a ponytail and her clothes were old and out dated. It had been years since she was able to buy anything for herself. Every payday she gave her check to Frank. She didn't dare to take anything out because he calculated everything down to the last penny including the amount that was owed to Uncle Sam. He was a genius when it came to math. Instead of hustling he could've been an accountant, but he loved the lifestyle. He didn't care what he hustled as long as he was making money. She was a runaway when she met Frank. Being seventeen years old, she had no idea what the streets had to offer. But anything was better than the abuse she suffered at home. I guess Uncle Doug touching me was better than getting my ass beat every day.

Frank was the perfect gentleman when they met and she didn't mind working the streets for him. He looked after all of his cookies. As he often referred to the women he was tricking. He took me under his wing instantly and agreed that I could stop working for him. Well that was after I did one last trick that almost killed me. This man was crazy and into some sadistic shit. Against my better judgment I let him tie me up and he started choking me as he fucked me. If Frank didn't come in the room when he did I wouldn't be here today. I always felt like I owed him my life. Frank still had his other cookies working for him but none of them could bring in the money like I did. Frank took me off the streets so I could just stay home but that was not working for me, I would be in the house all day with no one to talk to. It was driving me crazy and I needed something to do. I found a temp job that only paid ten dollars an hour. That wasn't any money living in Atlanta but Frank was still taking care of me.

Standing in the hallway she stood in shock. The house looked like a tornado went through it. Dishes were piled high in the sink, the living room smelled like feet and ass. Clean and dirty clothes were thrown all around in every damn room. Every day she came home the house was in this condition. Frank purposely made the house dirty so she could have extra work to do. It was all about control with Frank but there was nothing she could do about it. Grabbing a large trash bag she immediately started throwing away half eaten food Frank had all over the kitchen. She even found some food in the bathroom. Who the hell eats in the bathroom? This will take forever but I have to get it done before he comes home. Shit and I have to fix dinner. Not sure why he wants dinner because he won't be back home until tomorrow morning. I dare not ever ask him where he was at. The last time I did that he beat me so bad I stayed out of work for almost a month. Since I was the only one working he made sure I got better real quick so I could go back to work. That was the only time I remembered Frank being nice to me. He catered to me by fixing breakfast in bed, giving me flowers and running my bath water. Once I was back on my feet he started beating my ass again but this time he made sure not to beat me as badly.

His new trick is making him a lot of money for him. She is fine and I heard she keeps the men coming back for more. Hell she must be doing back flips or something because she is at the top of the list. He calls her Miss Honey and I can see why. My little paycheck shouldn't mean anything to him but he's a greedy bastard. He has so many Coogie, Black Label, and Sean John outfits now they can't fit in the closet. I wish he would fall in love with her and leave me the hell alone. My days of being jealous are long gone. When I was having sex with other men he never beat me but once he started getting high, and drinking things changed. He was arrested for trying to sell dope and one of his tricks to an undercover cop. He only spent five years in prison but whatever happened to him in jail changed him forever. He smacked me before but nothing like the ass beatings I've been getting lately. Once he was out of jail his personality changed. Like a fool I stayed by his side because he was the only family I knew. I should have left and never looked back. Frank had a million ways to hustle but none of them were bringing in any money. All of his other tricks left him when he got locked up and he hated the fact I didn't want to work the streets anymore. His last scheme was getting me to set up men while he robbed them. That didn't last long; in fact it back fired when one dude pulled a gun out and robbed us. *Oh well no time to keep dwelling on the past. I have to live for the future and that starts with cleaning this damn house. Hopefully I will have a moment to myself.*

After cooking and cleaning Suga finally had a moment to herself. It was almost 9 o'clock by the time she finished cleaning and fixing dinner. After taking a hot shower she sat down on the bed with her laptop. With Troy still on her mind she pulled his card out of her purse. After typing in his website www.troythetrainer.com over a dozen pictures popped up of Troy. There he is with that smile and body. Looking at all of his pictures, she used her index finger to trace over his body. She read his Bio and was checking out some of the pictures he had with celebrities. She realized he was a very successful trainer. He probably has a dozen women chasing after him. I wish I could be one of his women. Looking at a picture of Troy with no shirt and his hands were hanging slightly down by his sides. Sugar unwrapped the towel from her naked body as she lay back and fantasized about Troy. As she lay back on the bed she imagined feeling his touch. Gliding her hands over her body starting with her breast and making her way down to the sweet-filled sugar between her legs. With one hand she caressed her breast as she put her fingers inside her honey pot until they filled her up. Her body moved up and down as she pushed her hand further inside wanting him more. Her fantasy was interrupted when her computer started beeping. She looked at the screen and there was a message from Troy. Not realizing his webpage was interactive, Suga read some of the conversations he was having when he sent her a message:

Hello, welcome to my interactive web page. I see you are new and I would like to greet

all of my potential clients. Do you exercise or have any questions for me?

Damn, he loves his job she thought. After a brief pause of not saying anything he was about to disconnect. *Well if you have any questions I am here to give you the answers you need to get you started and help you stay healthy. Again welcome!*

Suga: Hi Troy it's Suga B. I bumped into you today and you gave me your card.

Troy: Oh that's right, Ms. Suga B. I remember bumping into you thinking heaven sent an angel my way.

Suga: Sure you did.

Troy: Honestly you are beautiful.

Suga: Thank you.

Troy: So are you going to take me up on my offer and get your free training classes? Suga: I may try to stop by on Wednesday.

Troy: Great I will make sure to give you my undivided attention. So what do you think of my web page.

Suga: I like it especially your pictures, you are very photogenic.

Troy: Thanks I used to model but decided my true passion is training.

Suga: Not to get in your business but do you make a lot of money training?

Troy: Yeah I make a good living. I have a lot of celebrity clientele.

Suga: I saw some of your pictures. I may have to change my career path.

Troy: Well it is a good career especially since people are trying to get in shape and eat healthy. You don't need any help considering you already have a beautiful figure.

Suga: Thanks, so what time is the class again?

Troy: The classes are after work starting at 5pm.

Suga: That maybe a problem, my boyfriend and I share the car and he has to be at work by 6pm.

Troy: Well maybe I can meet you for lunch around 1pm, I can at least show you the basics to help you keep up that hour glass figure.

Suga: Okay well I will see you on Wednesday.

Troy: Do you have an email or phone number so we can keep in touch?

Reluctantly she gave Troy her information...email and phone number.

Troy: Talk to you soon.

Suga started thinking of a way she could make it to more of his classes but realized Frank wouldn't believe anything she said. If I'm a minute late he questions me. Being an hour late he would probably tell me to quit my job. Too much to think about right now, I better go to sleep; it's already midnight. Suga laid in bed tossing and turning trying find the perfect spot to fall asleep but her body wanted Troy. Signing

back into her computer just to take another look at Troy she got an IM message.

Troy: Are u still awake?

Suga: Yes I'm wide awake. I couldn't sleep.

Troy: Me neither I kept thinking about you Ms. Suga B. Are you at home alone?

Suga: Yeah my boyfriend is at work.

Troy: Good, do you have a camera on that computer because I would love to see your pretty face?

Suga: Yeah.

Troy: Well sign in so I can see you.

She ran to the bathroom taking the du-rag off her head; her hair fell down to her shoulders. She wanted to look natural but added a little gloss to her lips. "Here I am." she said still nervous about talking to another man in Frank's house. "There is that beautiful woman I met earlier today." It had been a long time since someone called her beautiful. Troy was in front of the camera with no shirt on almost like the picture on his website. "Mmmm," she said thinking out loud. "Do you like what you see?" Troy asked

"I'm sorry, yes you are a very sexy man." "Thank you. Well I've shown you my body now can I see yours." "Excuse me?" "I want to see your body so I can tell you what you need to work on."

"I don't have on any clothes right now." "I thought you were asleep?" he asked. "I was but I sleep in the nude." His eyes got big like a kid in a candy store. "Well I guess that means I will have to get naked as well." He stood up in front of the camera as he took off his boxer briefs. His dick fell almost down to his knees. Suga imagined herself sitting on his dick as her clit started beating faster and faster like it had a brain of its own. "Well, I'm waiting." Troy said. "Okay are you sure this is just about working out?" "It can be about whatever you like." She stood up in front of the camera to make sure he had a full view of everything. He told her to turn around. She turned around in the middle of the floor with a sexy twirl. When she looked at him he was holding his dick like he was keeping it from coming through the camera. "Do you like what you see?" she said while making a kissy face.

"Yes, I do, and you have an amazing body. You sure you don't work out?" "Nope I just watch what I eat." "I can't wait until our first training session, because I am definitely going to give you a good workout." "What type of workout do you have in mind?" she asked flirting. She had to put a towel between her legs so her juices that were flowing wouldn't mess up the sheets. Suga B. I would love to come and work out with you right now. I hope I'm not crossing the line, but my dick is so hard right now. I may get blue balls tonight just thinking about you."

She put the laptop between her legs so he could get a better view of her moist warm spot. "What do you want to do to me first?" she asked. "I will kiss all over your body." Her eyebrow raised it sounded intriguing. "What time will he be home?" "Not until tomorrow morning." "I gotta have you right now," he said, as Suga yelled, "Me, too," with excitement. "How long will it take you to get here?" After giving him her address he said, "I can be there in about 20 minutes." He was putting his clothes on as they were talking. "Okay, I will see you then."

Suga decided to put on her red stilettos as she sat naked waiting for Troy. *What am I doing?* she thought. Frank will probably kill both of us but my body is craving for Troy. It's been so long since I've had sex. My pussy will probably run and jump on his dick before I even get up. She heard a car pull up and saw it was Troy. She went downstairs and opened the front door with nothing on but her birthday suite. She was ready to put him under her spell. She grabbed his hand and led him to her lair. Troy didn't resist as he followed her lead. She took him in the bedroom where the fireplace was on and the silk sheets were rolled back.

"Come here," he said grabbing her around the waist. "You are one sexy lady. So tell me what would you like me to do to you first?" *Whatever you want*, she thought; her body is just craving for a man's touch. He placed her body gently on the bed as he leaned over to kiss her softly around her neck then down to her breast. Suga closed her eyes enjoying the way he made her body feel. His touch was so gentle she fell into complete submission as he massaged her breast sucking each nipple with such intensity. Frank had never made her body feel the way Troy did. With her eyes closed, she felt his soft wet kisses on all of her erogenous zones as he made his way down to her sweet honey pot. He began to kiss her vertical lips. Suga moved her legs further apart so he would not miss any area down below. He was in his own private world as his tongue stroked over the head of her clit. With the tip of his tongue he licked the area between her vagina and anus darting his tongue in and out of her pussy. Suga's body was shaking and jumping with excitement as she started having multiple orgasms. He stood up rubbing his dick in his hands. When she finally opened her eyes he was getting on top of her.

Troy spread her legs further apart as he struggled to get his thick shaft deep inside of her. He gently slid all 12 inches inside as Suga let out an intense moan. Her entire body was shaking as Troy thrust his dick deeper inside. All you heard was a smacking motion from her wet pussy slamming against his shaft. Troy was going deeper and harder as they both yelled out in a rage of passion. Troy collapsed on top of her. Still laying between her legs, Troy started kissing softly on her body as he made his way back up towards her lips kissing her deeply. They both lay in the bed motionless enjoying each other's touch.

When Troy finally got up to leave around three in the morning, Suga didn't want him to leave. She was lost in his embrace but she knew he had to go. "Am I going to see you again?" she asked. "Baby I wish I could see you every day like this, so I guess that would be up to you."

CHAPTER 2

Suga woke up early in a good mood to fix breakfast for Frank as she waited for him to come home with her car. It was already 7am and he had not made it home yet. She didn't want to be late for work. Against her better judgment she called his cell phone. She was nervous because Frank told her to never call his phone if it wasn't an emergency. Well maybe he won't be mad; after all I need my job so we both can have somewhere to live. "Why the fuck are you calling me?" "I'm sorry, baby, I was worried." "Open the fucking door, stupid bitch!" He came in the house pissed. "Suga, I told you only to call me if it was an emergency," he said smacking her in the face. "I'm sorry I didn't want to be late for work." "What did you say?" he asked in a hostile voice. She cried as she stumbled to get the words out, "I'm sorry sir." "Now give me my damn breakfast and take your ass to work."

She went to fix his plate and looked at the rat poison she had under the sink. She was tempted to put some in his food. Sucking her teeth, *if I did it I'll be in jail and that bastard would probably still be alive,* she thought. She handed him his plate and left for work.

Suga sat in the car trying to get herself together before she went in the building to work.

Her hair was messed up and mascara was smeared on her face from her tears. I should just leave and go to a women's shelter but he would find me. She noticed Troy pulled up in the parking deck. Hoping he didn't see her, she sat in the car. Troy spotted her and waived as he walked toward her car.

"Good morning, beautiful." She smiled and kept walking. "Are you okay, Suga?" he asked grabbing her arm. "Yes I'm okay." He looked at her and rubbed her face. "What happened? Did he find out about last night?" "I don't want to talk about it right now." "Meet me at my car for lunch," he

99

said and then let her go. "Okay," as she walked in the building. When she got to her desk she looked in the mirror and noticed the red mark across her face. Oh God what lie can I think of if he ask me what happened. I'll just tell him I ran into a door. Suga kept watching the clock until it was time for lunch. I know he is going to ask what happened to my face. Do I tell him the truth or a lie?

Here I go she thought as she stepped out of the elevator. Troy was standing by his car smiling holding one red rose. She wanted to melt when she saw him. He handed her the rose, "Wow you have a beautiful smile," he said. "Thank you." "So what do you want anything to eat?" "No, I'm not hungry."

"I figured you would say that and as your personal trainer I am demanding you eat something so I bought you a shake. Let's get in the car and talk," he said opening the car door. Suga felt like a princess.

"Why are you being so nice to me?" "Because I like you and after last night, you are all I've thought about. So, how long have you been with your man?" "Honestly I've lost count and don't want to talk about him." "Did he put that mark on your face? ""No, I ran into the door." He looked at her and knew she was lying, but didn't press the issue.

"Excuse me," he said as he reached across her to look in the glove compartment. Suga not knowing what came over her, grabbed him into a kiss. His lips were soft like last night. "Come on, let's get out of this hot ass car. I want to show you my studio upstairs." Suga was standing by the the elevator when Troy grabbed her hand. "We are taking the stairs." "What? In these heels boy you crazy." "Walking up the stairs is a good workout even in stilletos." Half way up the steps Troy grabbed her and they shared a passionate kiss. Both of their hearts were pounding fast as she grabbed for his private area. Troy grinded his private part against her while pulling up her skirt. Pressing her body against the staircase door, he fumbled to pull his dick out of his pants while pulling her panties to the side. She put one leg up on his shoulder as his dick lead him to her warm spot. They both were in a heat of passion as their bodies moved together like a tidal wave in the ocean. He felt her lips clinched tight around his shaft as he started to cum. Suga could feel their juices dripping down her legs but her body still wanted more. He didn't say anything as he looked deep in her eyes. "You feel so good; I don't want to move," he said.

"Me neither but I have to get back to work. I guess I will show you the studio another day." She kissed him and walked away feeling like a different woman.

CHAPTER 3

The remainder of the day at work Suga was walking on a cloud. She daydreamed about Troy until it was time to leave for the day. She couldn't believe what just happened between them in the staircase, but she didn't regret it. It had been years since someone made her feel the way Troy did. The thought of going home made her sick. On her ride home she was singing in the car until she pulled up to her house. *I need to wipe this smile from my face because Frank will know something is wrong.* She walked in the house and it was in the usual cluttering chaos, with dishes piled high in the sink and stuff thrown everywhere. Surprisingly Frank was in a good mood as he came downstairs and kissed her on the cheek. He was dressed in a black suit and his Stacey Adams shoes. *That would be a nice suit to bury him in* she though. He was singing, "Were into money, were into money! Sweets I'm gonna get paid big tonight." *It's been a long time since he called me Sweets.* Not saying or do anything that may piss him off she made sure to look down at the ground. "How do I look?" he asked. "You look very handsome, sir." "That's right, I do look handsome." She handed him the keys. Extending his hand, "did you get the money I asked for? "Yes sir," she said handing him a $100 bill. *Well that was all the money I had left until payday next Thursday, and it's only Friday.* Frank left the house without saying goodbye.

Suga looked around and decided not to clean the house. She went upstairs to take a shower. Her body was still yearning to feel Troy's touch as the water ran down her body. The house was still a mess but Suga didn't care anymore. She texted Troy but he never responded back. Pulling out her laptop she checked to see if he was online. *I wonder where he could be?* Laying on the bed she started thinking about Troy. Her body yearned to fell his touch again. She pulled out her toy from underneath the mattress. She kept her toy a secret from Frank. The butterfly dildo helped to keep her sanity, especially living with Frank. The vibrator was helping to supply her needs, and her body fell into a trance when the loud banging at the door pulled her right out. Jumping off the bed, she quickly put her toy back in its hiding place and put on some sweatpants on to answer the door. It's probably Frank. He is going to be pissed because the house isn't clean and he is more than likely drunk. As she opened the door, Yasmine fell in the door way crying and bruised.

"You have to help me! He's going to kill me!" Yasmine sobbed. "Calm down, Yasmine. What happened?" "He is drunk. The deal didn't go the way he planned so he started yelling and going off beating me." "Where is he at?" "I'm not sure but I didn't have anywhere else to go." Yasmine's clothes were torn and blood was smeared all over her face. "He probably won't be home until later. Go and get cleaned up," Suga instructed.

Yasmine was new to the game but she was a pro at screwing every man she met. Hell, she fucked half of Atlanta ruining most of their lives and relationships. And her fiancé took all of her money. Photos of her were all over Atlanta from the AJC to being posted on mailboxes and storefronts. She was a prominent career woman, but once news about her sex affairs got out no one wanted to deal with her. Not sure how she met Frank but I should have forewarned her in the beginning. Yasmine came out of the bathroom looking tired and worn. She laid back on the bed and started crying. "Are you okay?"

"Yeah I'm just tired. My entire world has been turned upside down." "Yasmine you are a very beautiful woman. You don't have to live this lifestyle or put up with Frank. Unlike myself I have no choice but to deal with his bullshit." "Girl I am broke. I was robbed of half my money and the rest I tried to live off." Suga started to feel sorry for Yasmine as she lay down beside her. Face to face the two looked at each other as if they were reading each other's mind. Suga slid closer as she kissed Yasmine's bruises on her hands and face. She knew Yasmine needed to feel the way Troy made her feel. Yasmine didn't resist as the two embraced in a kiss. Suga maneuvered herself on top of Yasmine while unwrapping her body from under the towel. Yasmine's succulent breast stood at attention as Suga planted soft kisses around her nipples. Their bodies were moving together like a wave as Yasmine opened her legs wider to feel Suga's leg pressed on her clit. Taking off her sweat pants and tank top, Suga was ready to give Yasmine the release she needed. Her valley spread wider as Suga begin licking her sweet juices. Suga placed small kisses from her back to her breast. Yasmine couldn't move as her back begin to arch up every time Suga hit that special spot. Suga spread Yasmine's legs wider apart as she placed her clit on top feeling it pulsating. Yasmine's eyes rolled around in her head as Suga pressed her clit down harder. The two were mixing their juices like plutonium for an atomic bomb as they both exploded.

Exhausted from the felicity they feel asleep beside each other naked. Neither of them heard when Frank came in the house. With his eyes bloodshot red he stood in the doorway looking at the two of them with hate in his eyes. He took off his belt and began beating both of them out their sleep. They woke up startled, scared and screaming."What the fuck are you doing! Get your asses up! Frank yelled. "You bitches should be making me money but instead you fucking each other! He beat both of them unmercifully but Suga felt most of the blows because she was trying to protect Yasmine. As she tried to run Frank grabbed her hair and dragged her in the bathroom. "Bend over!" "Frank, please, I'm sorry!" "I said bend the fuck over! He hit her with the belt on her ass like she was a child being punished by her father. She tried to run again but Frank grabbed her arm, twisting it behind her. He beat her until she crawled up in a fetal position. Yasmine wanted desperately to help Suga but when Frank came out of the bathroom it was her turn as he beat her unconscious.

CHAPTER 4

Suga wanted desperately to talk to Troy and tell him what happened, but Frank wouldn't let her leave the house. He tied Yasmine up in the spare bedroom and only let her out when it was time to work the streets. Every time Troy called she couldn't answer the phone because Frank was around. Realizing Yasmine wasn't bringing in enough money he made Suga go back to work. But he dropped her off and picked her up from work every day. On her first day back to work she couldn't find Troy. She went by his gym but a note was on the door saying he was out of town. She called him from work but he never answered her calls.

Four weeks went by when she finally spotted Troy's car at lunch. She began to smile as she ran up the stairs to his gym. The door was unlocked but the lights were dim. She walked in and heard some noise. Troy was in the gym fucking another woman. She stood in shock for a minute as her heart dropped. She left out the gym feeling used and numb. Sitting at her desk Suga starred out of the window wishing she could fly away when an email popped up from Troy... *meet me in the parking deck.* At first she was hesitant but agreed because she was curious about what he had to say. He was sitting on his car when she came down to the parking deck. Suga didn't smile, only looking at him with an intense hate in her eyes.

"Hey beautiful are you okay?" "Yes, I'm just tired." "Sorry I didn't get a chance to call you back I've been out of town." "Yeah, I saw the sign on the door." "Are you okay?" "I just have a headache and have to go; Frank will be here to pick me up any second." She left Troy standing by his car with a puzzled look on his face. "Did I do something to you Suga?" "No, I just have a lot on my mind." It was already 5:30pm as Suga sat outside waiting for Frank to pick her up. *Where in the hell he could be?* she thought.

"Are you okay Suga?" asked her boss. "Yes, I'll be fine. The car broke down but he will be here soon," she said lying. It was 6:00pm and still no word from Frank. She started walking to the bus stop when Troy pulled up, hey beautiful lady do you need a ride? Too embarrassed to tell him Frank didn't pick her up from work she broke down crying. Troy immediately got out of his car to console her. Look you don't have to go back home, you can stay with me. Surprised by his response she was about to give him a hug when Frank sped around the corner. With fire in his eyes he jumped out of the car.

"What the fuck are you doing bitch? And who the fuck is this nigga you talking to? Frank you never came to pick me up and he offered me a ride." "Get yo ass in the car, Sweets!" "Hey, man, you don't have to talk to her like that!" "Look, this ain't none of your business playboy." "Get your ass in the car." Suga stood by the passenger door as Yasmine opened the door. Suga got in the back seat as they sped off. Troy was still standing outside as they drove away. Suga wanted to look back but was afraid Frank would notice. "Next time wait your ass outside until I come pick you up!" "Yes sir." "And when are you going to handle your business?" asked Frank. "Soon, sir, real soon." "Good because that little ass check you been bringing home lately is not enough." Frank dropped Suga off at home as he drove away with Yasmine still in the car.

She opened the door and was greeted by the usual disaster in the house. Standing in the middle of the living room she started screaming and throwing things around. It didn't make any difference because the house was already a mess. That bastard has abused me for the last time! She sat down thinking of ways she could kill Frank. I could poison him but that would leave traces in his system. Her phone was vibrating with a dozen messages from Troy. She called him back, "I'm sorry about tonight."

"I just wanted to make sure you were okay. Is he abusing you Suga?" "Not all the time we have our moments." "Any man that hits a woman is less than a man. Do you understand that? Why did he call you Sweets?" "That is just a nickname he has for me." "I want to see you tonight." Suga didn't say anything as the image of him having sex with another woman popped in her head. "Ok can I come to your place?

"Yeah that would be cool. I just don't want you to get in any trouble." "He won't even know I'm gone."

"Okay here is the address, 3-3-1-5 Saint Claire Drive. I will see you soon."

CHAPTER 5

Suga wanted to look sexy for Troy as she put on her sheer, white chiffon, baby-doll lingerie with her breasts out. The cab was waiting outside as she put on her trench coat. She left the house in the same condition it greeted her. When the cab dropped her off in front of Troy's house she thought she had the wrong address. She checked her phone and saw the address was the right one. Before she could ring the doorbell. Troy was opening the door for her. Hey I saw the cab pull up. He helped her take off her trench coat, "Damn, baby, you look good."

Suga walked around his house like she owned the place. "You have a nice house. I've always dreamed of living in a place like this. You must be rich?" "You could say that." She walked over to him, grabbing his dick. "You must be horny?" she asked. "Yep, I have an amazing appetite for you. Come on let's go upstairs." Suga pushed Troy back on the bed. "Can I tie you to the bed?" "Baby you can do whatever you want to me." Straddling him she kissed him grabbing his arms as she pulled out the handcuffs to cuff him to the bed. She rubbed his chest kissing him softly on the neck and playing with his nipples. Teasing him she grinded her ass on his dick. Troy was intrigued by her take-charge attitude. She pulled out his thick shaft and started stroking it with her hand. She licked his shaft with her tongue like it was her personal lollipop as she sucked the tip. "Damn, baby" was the only thing he could say. "Take these cuffs off so I can fuck you real good." "No, I told you I'm handling everything tonight." His dick was sticking straight up as she slid her sticky honey pot up and down his shaft. Suga was fucking him so good he came within seconds. "I'm thirsty," she said. "What do you have to drink?" "I have some vitamin water in the refrigerator." Suga went to get something to drink as Troy struggled to free

107

himself from the handcuffs. "You can take these off now." Suga ignored him as she walked around his bedroom opening his drawers and closets like she was searching for something. "Baby, what are you looking for?"

"Nothing just trying to figure out the type of man you really are."

"I'm whoever you want me to be. But I see you must like roll playing because you are into to some freaky shit tonight." "This is no roll play, Troy. This is real life." "Suga. you are crazy. Now take these handcuffs off of me. I'm sure your man will be home soon looking for you." Just then Frank appeared in Troy's doorway. "Here I am!" he said. "What the fuck is going on and why are you in my house?" "I think you hit the jackpot this time Sweets," Frank said to Suga. "Yeah, I saw the safe in the closet," said Suga. "You, bitch! All of this for some money! Just to rob me?" Troy yelled. "Hell yeah, Sweets is a bad bitch. This whore has been robbing niggas for years with that sweet ass pussy," Frank said. Troy was still struggling trying to get the handcuffs off as he watched Suga put his money and jewelry in an overnight bag. "I am really sorry, Troy, but I did like you a lot." "Shut the fuck up!" Frank yelled. "I don't understand. What about the marks on your body? I thought he was beating your ass?!"

"Man, like I said my hoe is good," Frank said. "She's been doing this to men for years. Did you think it was an accident when she bumped into you or when she fucked you real good on the first night? This shit is her second job. Hell it's easier than standing outside on the curb waiting for her to get that money.

"Is this true Suga?" Troy asked. She never said anything as she continued putting his jewelry in a bag.

"Look, man, think of this as payback for getting all that sweet wet pussy for free. As for beating her ass, shit sometimes she deserved an ass whipping." "Man, fuck you! Ya'll ain't going to get away with this. I know where you work and live Suga." "Man by the time you get up, we would've moved to another state. Ain't that right baby? "Yes, sir." "I don't believe this shit! You two will get yours!" "Shut the fuck up and stop whining! You got what you wanted from Sweets and now it's time to pay up," said Frank. "Sweets take that bag down to the car."

As she walked out Yasmine was coming up the stairs. Her face was bruised and she was crying.

"Where are you going?" Suga barked at her. Yasmine just kept walking like a zombie and never responded. As Suga reached the last step she heard shots. Suga dropped the bag and went running back up the stairs. Yasmine was standing over top of Frank ... *Pop! Pop! Pop! ...* she let off the entire clip. She dropped the gun and fell down screaming, "I hate you! I hate you! I hate you!" Troy shrieked, "Oh shit! What the fuck!" "Yasmine, what did you do?" Suga said as she ran over to her. "That was not the plan."

"I snapped," Yasmine answered. With her head in her hands Yasmine then said "I got rid of our problem." Troy was in shock and too scared to breathe or move a muscle. He wasn't sure if he would be the next victim. "Yasmine, I thought we decided to follow the plan. And play this whole thing out, taking what we needed and leaving Frank here, not killing him. I told you he would make me bring the stuff out to the car. This is why I said just stay there. We could be long gone by now."

Troy decided to break his silence, "What is going on? I don't understand." Yasmine protested, "Monica I just couldn't take it anymore, he was hurting me and you, what else was I suppose to do?" I wasn't sure what the next move would be as I looked at Troy. "Who is Monica?" he yelled. "Please tell me what is going on?" *Damn, he doesn't deserve this* I thought while walking toward him. "I am Monica," she said while sitting beside him on the bed. I am a professional con artist, which is how I met Yasmine the first time. I helped ruin her life. But Frank found her begging for help and brought her home. When she realized who I was, she was going to call the police but I convinced her not to. I let her know I was very sorry for what happened to her and how I want to get away from all this bullshit. She wanted her life back and I wanted to start a new one. And since Frank came up with the plan to rob you that as our get away from him. While he was be in here talking shit to you we were going to drive off. "Now the plan has changed and I am so sorry this had to happen, but we have to get out of town. You are a wonderful man but I am what I am," Suga continued. "Are you going to free me now?" "I can't do that. Feeling remorseful, you know too much now." "Ok, Ok please don't kill me, "Troy begged. "You can take what you need and leave. I'll think of something to tell the cops. Suga leaned over to kiss Troy on the cheek then walked off.

"Let's go baby. I hear Texas is a good place to start over," Suga said grabbing Yasmine by her hand.

Coming soon

THE SAME

mzScorpion

Lavender

"LaLa, when are you coming to see me? You missed the last two shows. I want you to come to this one. I'm having a show in two weeks at the Jacob Javits Center after the art fair." My brother yelled through the receiver in my ear while I walked in McDonalds to get something to eat. I moved the cell away because he was so loud.

"C'mon Luke, I told you I will try to come. You know I hate to miss your shows but I might be on call that night." Luke is my twin brother and he models for Push It modeling agency in New York City. He has been in Blackmen, XXL, and Smooth magazines along with a few fashion shows. The hottest one was the Macy's billboard or at least that is what I think.

"LaLa you always say that and then don't show up." LaLa is my nick name from Luke. When we learned how to talk, Luke had the hardest time saying Lavender so he would say LaLa.

"Ok, listen I am on my way to the hospital now. I just stopped to grab some grub. When I get there I will check the schedule and see if I'm working that night, and if I am, I will request it off or switch for the morning shift. Is that cool with you?"

"Yes, please make sure you call me and let me know so I can get your ticket."

"Wait a minute! You don't already have my ticket? As you kidding me! What if there are none left?"

"Relax you big baby. I have one but if you not coming I was going to give it to my new friend."

113

I could hear the smile in his voice, "Whatever Luke, I'm coming so don't play yourself. I come before any chick."

"Blah, Blah, Blah. Calm down, just make sure you call me once you got your information OK. I love you."

"Love you, too, Twin." Then I hung up.

I walked to the register and ordered a number three with ketchup only. I paid the girl then moved to the side while my food was being prepared. I decided to call Denver to see what he was up too since I left the house before he got home. I know he said he was going out for drinks with his boys later tonight so I wanted to say hi before he headed out. Denver is my boyfriend. We met in the hospital cafeteria about a month ago. I'm an intake nurse and he was visiting a friend. He claimed he would leave me alone if I gave him my number.

I pressed the green call button and listened as Denver's phone rang but he did not pick up. Just the voice mail: "You reached me but I missed you so do what you do best...HOLLA," *Beep.*

"Hey babe it's me? ... *Who else would it be?* "I was just calling to say hi before I got to work. I'm guessing you in the shower so I will see you in the morning." I ended the call as the girl placed my food in front of me on the tray.

"Thank you," I said and took the tray to find a seat. There were four seats together by the back door ... nice for me because no one was over there. I sat down, added ketchup to my fries and picked up my burger when a foul stench filled my nostrils. I looked up and noticed a lady walking around asking people for money. She looked horrible. You could tell she was on some form of drugs because her teeth were missing, her hair was thin and her cheeks were sunken in. She was scratching and sweating, and mind you, it was freaking mid-November, cold as hell out.

I had to look away because she was making me want to cry. I put my head down so I could finish my food. I bit into my burger and I could taste the funk...I flung my head up and she was standing in front of me, that women.

"Excuse me miss but can you spare some change?"

"Sure." I dug in my purse and pulled out a few coins and put them on the table and then pushed them toward her. She gave me a funny look, then she said, "thank you," grabbed the change and proceeded to walk off.

"Are you hungry?" I asked her.

"Oh, yes," the lady replied.

You can have my food if you like. I'm not going to finish it now. I pushed the tray toward her. She sat down and I got up. The stench coming from her body made me lose my appetite, but I knew she had to be hungry. I smiled and walked out making my way to the subway. Right before I entered my cell went off.

"Hello."

"Hey babe, sorry I missed your call, but I'm just getting off work and going to BW3's with the guys for drinks and shit."

"Oh ok, that is not a problem, I just wanted to say hi, have fun and a good night before I got to work. I miss you. Making a pouty face."

"Aww, I wish I would have seen you before you left for work then I could have fixed your sad problem."

"You so nasty," I told him with a big smile on my face. "You can make it up to me in that morning. But I have to catch my train so have fun and don't get in any trouble."

"Sure will and I won't, have a good night." Then the line went dead. I walked down the steps going uptown and swiped my metro card. The platform was packed. I really hate rush hour. I'm trying to get to work and all these damn people in my face...well they not in my face they just trying to get home. Mass transit sucks....Urgg.

I leaned against one of the street poles that has the street's name. I removed my I-pod and head phones, placed them in my ears and rocked to Mainos' "Hi Hater" until my train came. I rocked to my playlist all the way to work.

"Good evening, Lavender," my supervisor said when I walked up to the nurses' station.

"Hi Ms. Ula. How was your day?" She just smiled and flipped open a chart then started biting her pen top. I walked over to the staffs' board to see the schedule. I traced the calendar with my finger to locate my name for the date Luke is having his show...Yes I don't have to take off, I'm already off, but just to make sure I took a pen out my pocket and wrote my initials L.R. and the word off. Then I picked up the phone to call Luke. It rang then went to voice mail. I hung up and dialed back, I got the same response voice mail, beep... "Hey bro, just calling to let you know I am off the day of your show so make sure I have my ticket. OK don't make me hurt you. I'm just playing, anyway love you." I disconnected the line then checked the patient board to start my rounds.

Luke

I could see his silhouette through the smoke stain shower door. He was rubbing the loofa sponge over his chest and around his neck then back down chest to his crotch. My dick pulsated I was ready to jump in with him. Ooooo he just don't know what I wanna do to him or better yet what I want him to do to me. He continued to lather his body making sure to get every inch clean...good thing because I don't want to eat any chocolate raisins. I moved closer poking my lips out then pressing them against the glass making kissy noises.

He yelled, "wait your turn with your greedy ass!"

I licked the glass then laughed, "I will see you when you get out!" I walked out the bathroom and headed for the kitchen when I heard my cell buzzing, informing me of a message. *Chaaa* I sucked my teeth, who is calling me now? I went in the bedroom and picked up the phone off the night stand, I pressed the green phone icon so the power came on then I clicked the voice message button to listen. Of course it was Lala "Hey bro just calling to let you know I am off the day of your show so make sure I have my ticket ok, don't make me hurt you...I'm just playing anyway love you."

Cool I said to myself, then powered the phone off; I don't want any interruptions while I'm getting my dick waxed. I heard the shower turn off and door thud.

"Luke, what you cook for dinner I'm so hungry I could eat three men," Neek yelled from the bathroom.

"You better watch yourself I'm the only man you get to eat round here." We both started laughing. "You will see when you get out."

I went in the kitchen to make the plates.

Neek came in right behind me wow it smell real good in here. "What we having." "Spaghetti and meat sauce, Texas toast, and a side salad. You want a drink?"

"Sure thing, but heavy on the rocks you know how I like it."

I took a glass out the cabinet and added ice from the fridge door up to the rim then pour him some chocolate vodka from three olives. I swear that stuff smell just like candy. I gave him the glass along with a kiss on the lips.

"Why you kiss me before I had my drink? Now I don't want it because you taste better," Neek said smiling.

"Aw, you know just what to say to get me hard." I made our plates and sat down at the table with my boo. We ate and talked about my show that was in two weeks. "Are you gonna come to this one?" I asked him.

"I'm going to try. I will be with my dad that day. Remember I told you he has Alzheimer's so I try to make sure he sees a familiar face every week besides those nurses and doctors."

Neek is so sweet, and I love how he takes care of his father. Neek is my boyfriend and we met at a party one of my co-workers was having for his birthday. It is called a Sausage Party. Only men are invited. Neek was part of the entertainment.

I was on the sofa watching one of the dudes give head to the stripper when Neek came out, flipped upside down in front of my homeboy and let him eat his ass. That shit turned me the fuck on. He was on his head with his ass pressed against my friends face so I got on my knees in front of them and pulled my pants down placing my dick in Neek's mouth. I took his in mine maneuvering the tip of my tongue around the head, then tracing each vein as it pulsated.…

MONEY OVER EVERYTHING

Lynx

INTRO

Shelby

I remembered it like it was yesterday when my mom said my dad was dead. At the time it didn't register in my brain what she saying. I was only 15 when he was found dead in the alley behind our house on Fourth Avenue with a note that was written in his blood that said, 'debt paid'.

That morning started out like any other day, my mom was in the kitchen cooking breakfast for me and my daddy. My daddy normally stayed out late and didn't come home until the next morning. He didn't come home that night so we thought he was still out working. Someone came banging on our door. I ran to open it thinking my daddy forgot his keys, but when I opened the door I saw two white men in suits. My mom came to the door and told me to go upstairs. Instead I decided to walk to Siegel's the store down the street to get me a Big Ben juice and some funions for later. As I was walking to the store I saw police cars in the alley but didn't think anything of it because the police were normally in the area. A few people in the store were looking at me with a sad look on their face. I didn't pay any attention thinking maybe they were scared of my daddy. He wasn't a bully but he protected his family. When I got back to the house, my mom was throwing things around in the living room like a crazy woman. She was breaking everything, crying and screaming my daddy's name. I yelled at her asking what was wrong but she just broke down crying. She grabbed and hugged me really tight and whispered my daddy was dead. I stood there speechless not knowing what to say. A tear

119

rolled down my face and I let out the loudest scream that probably woke up the entire neighborhood.

Word of Dukey Blue's death spread quickly around the neighborhood. There were a lot of stories about who may have killed my daddy. Some people said other drug dealers had him killed, the mafia, he owed money to some Jamaicans, or one of his mistresses' boyfriends killed him. Anyone of the stories could have been true but I still missed my daddy. His friends tried to console us but my mom took it really bad. After the funeral we grew further apart. My mom didn't care about anything anymore, including me. She would stay gone for days or weeks without letting me know when she would be back. I stayed in that big house trying to keep my sanity. My neighbor Ms. Jacobs, who lived across the street, checked on me all the time. She made sure I had a home-cooked meal every night.

I found out my mom was getting high when we were being put out of our house. Our furniture was scattered all over the sidewalk when I came home from school. People had already rummaged through a lot of our things until Ms. Jacobs came home and started guarding it like a hawk. Back then we didn't need neighborhood watch because Ms. Jacobs knew everything that was going on in the neighborhood. Some of my dad's friends got a lot of our things back that were stolen but the rest was gone. I didn't care as long as they didn't take the pictures of my daddy. When my mom came home that day she was high and didn't understand what was going on. She even started taking off her clothes in the middle of the street thinking it was her bedroom. It was so embarrassing. My dad's friends were upset she didn't tell them she needed money for the rent. Although Dukey Blue was gone they were still going to look out for his family.

After staying with different people in the neighborhood I went to live with my mom's sister Aunt Gloria. My mom said she was going to rehab to get her life back together, and once she got out she would come get me. I wasn't close to Aunt Gloria, but she seemed like she was cool. She didn't have any kids so I'm sure the fact that she was getting a steady check each month made the deal even sweeter.

I didn't believe my mom would come get me after rehab because she wasn't strong enough to stop. Every time someone mentioned my dad's name or she saw his picture, she broke down crying. I lived with my Aunt Gloria for almost a year until her nasty ass boyfriend Tommy tried to rape me. I still get chills when I think about him touching me. Tommy was a bum. He didn't work and was drunk all the time. From the time I moved in with them he always had a slick grin on his face. You know the look some men have as if to say, "wait until I get you by yourself". I guess he thought I was a naïve little girl but he should've known because Dukey Blue made sure his baby girl knew how to handle herself. This one particular night my aunt was supposed to be working late. She left out the house about ten o'clock. I took my bath and got in the bed. Once I got in my room I always locked my door. I didn't trust Tommy or my aunt because she always came into my room taking my clothes. I was in a deep sleep having one of those dreams I didn't want to wake up from. I'm not sure how Tommy came in my room that night but he did. I woke up startled with his dirty ass hands on my mouth breathing in my ear. He sat on top of me holding my arms and pushing my legs apart. I screamed and struggled as I tried to keep my legs closed. He said, "You are gonna like what Uncle Tommy has for you." He managed to pry my legs apart, holding them down with his knees as he ripped my panties off. He was like a dog in heat as he fumbled to pull his dick out of his pants. I grabbed the knife I kept under my pillow as he struggled to penetrate my pussy. I was still a virgin and my first experience was not going to be of this drunken bastard raping me. I stabbed him right in the jaw, pulled it out and stabbed him again in the arm. He yelled as he jumped off of me falling to the floor. I quickly got off the bed and kicked him in his dick. Blood was everywhere as I ran toward him with the knife in my hand, tripping over the rug and stabbing him again in his leg. He ran out of the room holding his face and leg calling me a crazy bitch! If I had a gun he would've been dead, but my daddy always told me when you pull a gun on someone be prepared to use it.

My aunt who I thought was at work came running in my room not asking if I was okay but instead yelling, "What the hell did you do to him?!" I was half-naked on the floor crying. I told the bitch he tried to rape me. She gave me an evil ass look as she went to check on him. "You could've killed him with that knife! I gave you a place to live when your crack head mother couldn't take care of you and this is the thanks I get? Shit it's about time you learned that bills have to be paid and that shit between your legs was going to keep food on the table and keep the lights on. Damn, all Tommy wanted was a little pussy from you. You walk around the house flaunting your ass around my man; the least you can do is fuck him when he wants it! What, you think you are too good for Tommy? Hmmm, you just like you're stuck up ass momma! Get your

121

shit together and get the fuck out of my house! Come on Tommy so I can take you to the emergency room." Fat bitch didn't have to tell me but once. I was going to be gone by the time they came back from the hospital. I should've stabbed her for setting me up to be raped. I started packing my clothes and realized I didn't have anywhere to go or anyone to depend on except myself. I cried thinking *why did my daddy have to die?* He would have killed Tommy and Aunt Gloria for messing with his baby girl. I could always go back to my old neighborhood but I didn't have a phone number for anyone. With my luggage in my hand I walked to the bus stop. It was late and the buses stopped running, but I didn't want to be in that house. I used the payphone to call my best friend Towanda. It was almost three o'clock in the morning when I called her house crying. Her mom, Ms. Carolyn, immediately came to pick me up. I told her what happened and she was pissed. She told me I could stay with them for as long as I wanted.

Ms. Carolyn treated me like her daughter, something I was missing so much from with my real mother. She called the police the next day and pressed charges against Tommy. My aunt didn't like that at all; when she found out she came over Ms. Carolyn's house cursing and wanting to fight. Ms. Carolyn didn't back down. She was only 5'6" but she was a feisty woman. Aunt Gloria was cursing and yelling, but Ms. Carolyn was so calm. We were sitting on the porch, and Ms. Carolyn told me to hold her glasses. She took a sip of her lemonade and walked off the porch. Aunt Gloria was still yelling and screaming when Ms. Carolyn punched her in the face knocking her out cold. Everyone in the neighborhood laughed. Ms. Carolyn called the police and they arrested Aunt Gloria for trespassing. Ms. Carolyn still had it out for Tommy and couldn't wait to see him.

We were at Siegel's grocery store when I spotted Tommy standing at the bus stop. I told Ms. Carolyn that was Tommy and she told me and Towanda to go sit in the car. She walked up to him and they exchanged some words. Ms. Carolyn grabbed his dick and punched him in the face about two to three times. He fell to his knees crying because she wouldn't let go of his dick. When she finally let go she spit in his face. She came back to the car saying, "I hope you both remember that if a man ever hits you or tries to take advantage of you, always grab his dick first and make sure you get a good grip so you can bring him to his knees." A man can't think without his dick first. When I looked back Tommy was still on his knees crying. At that moment I knew Ms. Carolyn was not to be played with. In two days she beat two people that tried to hurt me. I stayed with Ms. Carolyn and Towanda until I graduated from high school. No one from my family was at my graduation except my dad's close friend High Pocket. He was a cool old man and always gave me money when I needed.

I hadn't heard anything from my mom, I wasn't sure if she was dead or alive. Once I turned eighteen I got my own apartment, and I've been on my own since that day....